ROCK

My

WORLD

(Black Falcon, #2.5)

MICHELLE A. VALENTINE

Chapter One

Aubrey

I uncross my legs and then cross them again in the opposite direction. Still uncomfortable, I shift in my seat. Plane seats aren't exactly known for being luxurious, but I thought sitting in first class would be way better than coach. Guess I was wrong.

I sigh and flip through the magazine I brought on board with me, trying to take my mind off what lies in wait for me at the end.

A deep laugh rumbles next to me and I whip my head in that direction.

"Nervous?" Zach teases while he offers me one of the Oreos he's eating.

I shoot him a look, which only causes his smile to grow wider. "No."

He wraps his arm around me and tucks my shoulder under the crook of his arm. "You forget how well I can read that little body of yours, Kitten. You afraid of what your parents will say when you bring me home to meet them?"

"Of course not," I fire back immediately.

I stare up at him as his green eyes search my face. His baseball cap is pulled down low on his forehead—his favorite public disguise since he's best known for his crazy blonde and black Mohawk—framing his handsome face perfectly.

I sometimes hate that he knows me so well. The truth is I *am* nervous, but I'm not about to admit that to him. My parents are the most uptight, conservative people on the planet. They have no clue their little girl is about to bring home a bad-assed, tattooed rock star. I want them to get along, even though I know the chances of that happening are slim to none. I probably should've eased them into the idea instead of springing it on them like this, but there wasn't any time. This trip isn't exactly just a visit, it's business too, and in my situation, father is the best person to ask for help.

"Attention all passengers, we will be landing in Houston shortly. Please bring your seats to an upright position and make sure your tray table is the upright, locked position..." The flight attendants instructions cause my heart to leap in my throat.

It won't be long now.

My parents have no clue I'm coming, let alone bringing a guest with me. It was Zach's idea to come here after the reality that I was now an unemployed new grad hit me. I cried for a solid week. It was like part of my soul had been torn away and my purpose had been yanked from me. Center Stage Marketing is a dream company to work for and I wasn't ready to give it up.

Granted what I had done to Isaac was wrong, but it had nothing to do with my work performance. Zach tried to convince me he could help me find another job, I wouldn't take him up on the offer though. I earned my degree on my own merit, and I want to find and keep a job the same way. The only sound thing that comes to mind is getting my old position back—via the legal route if I have to.

Zach takes my hand into his and I give his fingers a gentle squeeze. "Thank you for coming with me."

He smiles and presses the back of my hand to his lips. "Where else would I be? You need me? I'm there. It's you and me against the world now, right?"

I nod and stare up into his green eyes, taking in the fact again that this man truly belongs to me. "Absolutely."

The plane touches down and I Zach and I exit rather quickly, pulling our bags along with us through the airport terminal. We finally make it to the rental car area of the airport and luckily the gray-haired woman waiting on us has no idea who Zach is. The woman processes us through in a hurry while looking up to eyeball his arms with a snarled lip every couple seconds.

She's probably desperate to get rid of the tattooed hooligan at her counter.

Once we're in the parking garage Zach clicks the car fob and the lights blink on a blue Ford Fusion. "That's us."

I grip the handle of my suitcase and roll it towards the car. "It shouldn't take long to drive to my parent's house. They live just outside the city."

Zach pops the trunk and tosses his bag inside, following it with mine. "That's good. After spending most of my time on the road, I like short trips. Being cooped up for long periods at a time sucks—it's the one thing I hate about my job."

I frown. "I'm going to hate that part, too. I can't imagine being away from you so long."

Tattooed arms reach out and wrap around my waist. I smile as Zach pulls me in tight against his hard body, and I squeeze him back as I lay my head on his chest. "I wish you would take the opportunity to come on the road with me while you're between jobs. I would love to have you by my side."

"Zach…"

"I know. I know. I'm being a selfish jerk. The idea of missing you after I just got you back drives me crazy." He sighs. "I love you and I want to be with you every second that I can. Can you blame a guy for being obsessed with his beautiful, sexy, hell-raiser in the sack girlfriend?"

I giggle at how dream-like it is that he's just as crazy about me as I am about him. "You're ridiculous."

A deep laugh rumbles in his chest. "Ridiculous, maybe…honest, damn straight. Come on. We better not keep those parents of yours waiting."

I stiffen in his arms. "About that...I didn't exactly tell them we were coming."

I pull back and peek up at his face, afraid of the disappointment I'll see there. His lips pull into a tight line as he stares down at me. "So they have no idea they're about to meet me?"

I bite my bottom lip. "They don't even know I'm dating anyone."

This time I feel Zach's back stiffen against my fingers. It's tension I've created by not being honest with him about the situation.

He starts to pull away but I grab the hem of his shirt. "Zach. Stop."

He freezes in my grasp and tilts his head up—doing everything he can to not look at me. I study his strong jaw line and the slight stubble growing along it. I hate that I'm hurting him. Fighting with him is the last thing I want to do. I wish he could understand why I didn't say anything to them. He has no clue how hard it's going to be facing my parents and telling them how irresponsible I was in their eyes for dating this gorgeous rock star before me, throwing my career away in the process. My father doesn't believe in doing crazy things in the name of love.

How can I explain to Zach while I love him with every inch of my being, my father and his hard-ass ways still scare the shit out me even though I'm an adult? I know it doesn't make sense, but I still can't bring myself to succumb to my father's views on life in general.

I take a deep breath. I brought him here to make them understand. "I'm sorry. I should've told my parents, but I knew if I did over the phone they wouldn't get it. They wouldn't know how special you are to me. I wanted to introduce you in person and make them see."

Zack tips his head down and stares into my eyes before pushing my hair behind my ear. "I get it. Just because they're our parents doesn't make them the best people sometimes. I know that as well as anyone."

I lean into his hand that lingers against my cheek and think about how great my family life was compared to his. And how I'm being such a baby over things and he's still so understanding. "Thank you."

He smirks. "Besides, you probably didn't want your mom Googling me and seeing some pictures of her daughter's boyfriend in um…" He clears his throat. "Compromising positions."

I smack his arm. "Ugh. Gross."

He laughs as he walks to the passenger side door and opens it for me. "What? You don't think she needs a little man candy in her life? I'm sure she does after dealing with The Judge all these years."

I take a couple steps toward him while I groan. "My parents don't have sex, okay?"

Zach rests his hand on top of the door while I squeeze between it and the car and face him. "Of course they do. How else do you think you got here?"

My stomach turns at the thought of my parents that way. "Okay, so maybe they did it two times, but that's it—once for me and once for my brother. No more. "

He laughs and I scrunch my nose. Zach stretches out his index finger and taps me on the nose. "Wishful thinking, Kitten. Everyone has sex." I open my mouth to protest, but he quickly cuts me off. "*Everyone*. When we hit our fifties, we'll still be having hot, porn like sex every day. My stamina has no expiration date, babe."

When he wiggles his eyebrows a laugh escapes me. There's no doubt in my mind that this sexy beast before me will probably still have his most favorite body part standing to attention well into his golden years. It's just funny thinking of this wild man as ever being old. He's too strong willed and virile for me to picture him in any other state than he is right now—a tatted up rockstar with muscles galore.

I tug on the bill of his ball cap and then take my seat inside the car. "Come on, sex machine. You have some parents to impress."

"No worries. Moms love me." He winks at me after he shuts me in.

I shake my head. It's kind of gross that he's dead on. I've seen the way women throw themselves at my man. I've seen the cougars in full effect. Apparently, lust has no age limits.

Once we're on the road, I stretch my legs out and take in the familiar scenery that covers the landscape on my way to my childhood home in The Woodlands, in northern Houston. "Make a left here."

Zach let's out a low whistle as we finally pull onto my street. "Wow, looks like I'm dating a spoiled, little, rich girl."

"I'm far from rich. The Judge is the one that's loaded, not me," I remind him.

He shrugs nonchalantly. "Maybe so, but I guarantee you never went without." When I don't immediately have a snappy comeback to argue that I didn't have it made like he thinks, he smiles. "That's what I thought."

The truth is I *did* have it made as a kid—as long as I played by my parent's rules. I was never one really to push the boundaries the perfect child role they expected my brother and I to play, but I didn't fully embrace the uppity lifestyle, either—which probably explains why I started dating the bad-boys in college. They were so different from the guys I grew up with in high school. They hated rules and loved their freedom, and deep-down I discovered the same thing about myself once I was out in the real world and could make my own decisions.

Zach pulls into the drive and cuts the engine before turning his head my direction. "Anything else I need to know before I walk in there?"

My mind wonders through a few scenarios of how this first meeting could go down. The last boy I brought home was clear back in high school, and he was nothing like Zach. While my mother knows I tend to get my heart crushed by loser men, she's never had the pleasure of meeting my new type. She's used to seeing me with uptight jerks like Isaac, so I'm not sure how she'll react. I pray they remember their manners and are polite to him, whether they approve of our relationship or not. If not, I'm going to have to put on my big-girl panties and tell them to fuck off.

Not one piece of advice to give to Zach flits through my mind, but I want to reassure him as I hope for the best. "Just be your charming self and they'll love you."

He flicks his green eyes towards the large, two-story, brick home in front of us. "I can't get over the size of this place. Lawyers really make that much?"

"The good ones do." I touch his hand on the gear-shift. "Remember, my dad takes his job pretty seriously, so don't crack jokes about it. He actually likes it when my brother, Gabe and I call him The Judge like the rest of this town. That's how much he's into it. It's his life."

Zach raises his brow. "Maybe I should have you start calling me Guitar God. Might be kind of fun, especially in the bedroom. What do you think?"

I smack his arm. "I think you better keep dreaming, because that's so not happening."

He laughs as he opens his door. I take a second to appreciate the view when he walks around the front of the car. His jeans hang low on his hips, yet hug his butt perfectly, accentuating the curve, making it almost yummy enough for me to take a nibble. The white t-shirt he's wearing strains against his toned, tattooed arms as he reaches up and tugs on the hat that's hiding his trademark hairstyle. He's so freaking hot. How did I get this lucky?

Lost in the thought of how sexy he is, I jump and clutch my chest when he opens my door.

He stares down at me with those sparkling, green eyes with a perplexed expression. "You alright there?"

A blush fills my cheeks as I stand up. "Never better."

Zach wraps his arms around my shoulders and grins. I inhale the spicy scent of his cologne mixed with the soap he uses. "You were thinking naughty thoughts about me again, weren't you?"

I bite my lip but never tear my gaze away from the challenge in his eyes. "Maybe I was."

A growl escapes his lips as he pushes his hips against me, allowing me to feel the growing erection in his pants against my belly. "Damn it, Kitten. See what you do to me. I swear to God I'm on like a fucking light switch whenever thoughts of you and sex enter my head at the same time. You've ruined me for life."

I laugh and run my hands up and down his back. "I'm glad I've ruined you for all other women. I want to keep you all to myself."

"You don't ever have to worry about that, babe." He reaches up and tucks a strand of my auburn hair behind my ear. "If I have it my way, you'll be stuck with me forever."

His thumb traces my chin and he leans in and presses his lips softly to mine. My legs below me instantly turn to jelly and I sink further into him. It's amazing the affect a simple kiss from this man can have on me. It was one simple kiss from him that first night backstage that turned my world on its head and changed everything in my life. For him—for this love we have—I would do anything. This man is my world.

My lips part of their own accord and I allow his tongue to slip inside my mouth. I grip his shirt in my hands, holding on tight as I get lost in how much my body craves him.

Lean muscle pushes against me and I steady myself against the car for support. Zach's fingers thread into my hair and a small whimper escapes my lips when he pulls away. Feather light kisses run along the corner of my mouth before he works his way across my cheek to the spot just below my ear that drives me crazy. My head falls back as he runs a hand down my side.

We probably look semi-pornographic making out in my parent's driveway, but I don't care. Zach brings out a wild side in me even I didn't know existed—a true rebel willing to risk anything for the man who makes my body feel this good. His touch is pretty damn addictive.

He sighs against my skin. "We should probably go in before someone reports the tattooed man mauling The Judge's daughter to the cops."

"To hell with the neighbors," I breathe, not wanting to lose this feeling.

Zach chuckles. "As much as I would like to give the neighbors a hell of a show by fucking you on the hood of this car, I don't think it's the best idea. I actually want your family to like me."

My shoulders instantly sag. "You're right. It wouldn't be a good look, would it?"

He pulls his lips into a tight line and shakes his head. "Probably not. Besides, your father has enough connections to kill me and get away scot free if he were to catch me with my dick in his little princess."

I pinch his pierced nipple through his t-shirt. "You know exactly what to say to ruin a perfectly romantic moment. My father shooting you is the last thing I want to picture right now."

"Ouch!" He swats my hand away and then rubs his chest. "Oh, you're going to get it!"

Zach leans in and smiles playfully, ready to pounce on me and a voice behind us stops us both in our tracks. "Get *what?*"

I jerk my body to the right in order to peer around Zach's shoulder and see my brother behind him. "Gabe!" I scurry over to him and he scoops me up in a bear hug. "What are you doing here?"

Gabe laughs and tosses his shaggy, brown hair out of his blue eyes. "I could ask you the same thing, little sister."

He sets me on my feet. Gabe's filled out since I saw him last spring. The gleaming-white, tennis outfit he's wearing shows off the lean muscles in his forearms and toned calves. "Wow. You been working out?"

He shrugs. "A little. The ladies seem to like it."

I laugh. "Always the ladies man—you never change."

Gabe grins down at me. "Can't say the same thing about you, sis." His eyes flit over my shoulder in Zach's direction. "Who's this?"

I smile and then turn towards my boyfriend who's' watching us with mild curiosity while leaning against his rental car. "Gabe, this is my boyfriend, Zach. Zach, this is my brother, Gabe."

Zach pushes his sculpted body away from the car and extends his hand. "Hey, man. Nice to meet you."

Their hands make a small audible clap when they meet. "You, too. Say, you look familiar. Have we met before?"

My brother's eyes scan my man's tatted-up arms as he mentally tries to place his familiarity. While I know why Gabe thinks he's seen Zach, I won't burst in and ruin Zach's cover if he isn't ready to share that part of himself with my family, yet. I'll leave that secret for him to reveal.

Zach shrugs and grins wickedly. "Maybe at the country club?"

My bother pauses for a moment before he chuckles, catching the hint of amusement in Zach's voice. "I think I would remember you at the club. Hell, you'd be my biggest competition for the ladies. I know how they go gah-gah over men with tattoos."

I hook my arm through Zach's and peer up at his face. "I can vouch for most women when I say tattoos are sexy."

My brother shakes his head. "Let's hope you're right about that, sis, because he's about to meet a woman who I'm pretty sure has a snooty-stick shoved so far up her ass she doesn't find anything appealing, let alone sexy."

I smack my brother's arm. "Gross! Don't ever say Mom and sexy in the same sentence ever again. Those two words are now forbidden for use together."

Gabe laughs. "You know I never did like rules. We always had that in common, remember?"

I give Zach's arm a gentle squeeze, thinking of how I'm breaking the rules right now by bringing this man home. "I do. Are Mom and The Judge home?"

"Yeah, they're in there. They don't know you're coming do they? I mentioned you coming home this weekend and neither of them had no clue what I was talking about, so I left it alone. I figured you had your reasons."

I shake my head. "No. I didn't want to explain my unscheduled visit with them."

Gabe's eyes widen and instantly drop down to my stomach. "Holy shit! Are you pregnant?"

My hand flies to cover my belly. "God, no! "

"You're getting married then, or you've already gotten married?" My brother grins while his eyes bounce back and forth between Zach and me. "I'm glad I decided to come home from school this weekend. This should be a damn good show."

"You're an idiot." I sigh. "It's neither of those things…" My eyes flick to Zach's for a split second before I turn my attention back to my semi-annoying sibling. "At least not yet, anyway. But, there is something pressing I need to speak with them about."

Gabe waves us towards the house. "Well, come on. Let's get this show started. I have a court reserved in a bit with a hot, little blonde from the club. I'm hoping to crush her on and off the court, if you know what I mean."

I roll my eyes. "What is it with you men and sex? Is that all you ever think about?"

Both men in my presence answer "yes" in unison, and then immediately laugh.

"I think you and I are going to get along just fine, Zach. Watch out for my old man, though. In this case the apple falls very far away from the tree."

"Thanks for the tip, bro. I've heard some stories about The Judge," Zach says.

"Most are probably true. Tread softly, man. The tattoos won't help your case much, I'm afraid. He's old school and correlates them with criminal activity."

Zach shakes his head. "That's so judgmental. Talk about stereotypical."

My brother shrugs. "He is a judge. It's his job to be judgmental."

"Touché," Zach laughs. "Let me grab our bags from the trunk."

"I'll help you," Gabe says.

My heart warms instantly at the sight of the man I'm deeply in love with talking and laughing with my one and only sibling. More than anything in the world, I want Zach and my family to get along well. I know if they can see the way he loves me they'll understand why I love him so much and why he's the perfect man for me. Gabe's right though. The tattoos won't make the best first impression—neither will his occupation once they all find out who he is, but I hope they can get past that. I *need* them to get past that, because no matter if they approve or not, this is the man I'm going to spend the rest of my life with.

My brother takes my bag from the trunk and Zach closes the lid. "Anna nearly has dinner finished. You're just in time to sit down to a traditional Sunday lunch with the family, Zach."

Zach arches his pierced eyebrow. "Anna?"

"Our housekeeper," I answer after retrieving my purse from the car. "My mother hasn't cooked a meal herself since Dad's career took off."

"And that's a blessing if you ask me. Anna is a much better cook than Mom." Gabe states as we head towards the front door. "I prefer a little Latin flavor."

I smirk at him, knowing he's not just referring to food. "You mean you prefer Alandra, Anna's daughter."

Gabe stops at the door and grins while his free hand rests on the handle. "I haven't seen Alandra since she went away for college on the East coast." His eyes get lost, and almost have a dreamy appearance like he's remembering some long lost dream. "I wonder what she's up to? I bet she's hot now."

I shake my head and nudge his shoulder. "Come on, Romeo. Let us in."

The heavy, wooden door swings open with ease as soon as Gabe turns the handle. The house is just as immaculate as always. The gleaming, white tiles in the foyer make the double, grand staircases stand out against the stark walls. The round mahogany table between them matches the wood throughout the house perfectly, while the bright yellow and pink flower arrangement resting on its surface gives the room a pop of color.

"Wow," Zach says as he takes in the large space. "If *MTV* ever brings *Cribs* back and wants to come to my house, I'm bringing them here instead. This puts my place to shame."

"I'm sure it doesn't. I can't wait to see your place," I say.

A wide smile stretches across his face. "Soon."

The sound of high heels clicking against the floor catches my immediate attention and I stiffen. "Good land of the living, is that my Aubrey I hear in here?"

Mom appears in the room in a pink knee-length skirt and matching blouse, her pearls on display around her neck. Her auburn hair hangs loose above her shoulders, and as always she looks very put together. I smile as I set my purse on the table and step into her outstretched arms. "Hi, Mom."

She pats my back. "Darling, it's so good to see you. Let me take a look at you." She steps back and grabs each of my wrists, effectively spreading my arms away from my body for her once over. "Charles, dear, you must come greet our unexpected visitor!"

I freeze as my mom calls for my father to enter the room. In an instant, my father is there, dressed in his khaki pants and long-sleeved button down shirt—his typical casual Sunday outfit. His salt and pepper hair is neatly trimmed and styled like he's stuck in the eighties.

The Judge smiles. "There's my little princess. Why didn't you tell us you were coming, honey?"

I cringe at him referring to me as his princess. It only solidifies what Zach was saying earlier about me being spoiled.

"It's good to see you, Judge," I step into my father's awaiting hug.

"Dear, would you pay the poor cab driver so he can leave," Mom says to Dad while clutching her pearls, and I instantly jerk away from the hug.

"Here you go, young fellow." Dad reaches for his wallet and I shake my head placing my hand on his arm, stopping it mid-motion. "Don't be silly, Aubrey. I'll pay your fair."

Without warning the Judge takes a couple steps toward Zach and stuffs a wad of cash in his hand. Zach's eyebrows rise as he stares down at the money. My face heats up and I know it's fifty shades of red as I feel embarrassed that my family is so close-minded to think my man is nothing but a hired hand. I want to crawl into a hole and die.

I reach over and touch my father's shoulder. "No, Daddy. He isn't the cab driver. This is Zach, my boyfriend."

The Judge eyebrows pull together in confusion. "Boyfriend? Honey, I don't understand. Have you seen this man? I thought your mother and I raised you better than that."

"Daddy, please!" I scold my father while anger that he would treat the man I love this way boils inside me. I step to Zach's side and wrap my arm around his waist while he throws his arm over my shoulders. "I love him and I would appreciate if you could all to treat him with the same respect you show me. Besides, he's not some riff-raff off the street, he's—"

Zach holds up the hand holding the money, cutting me off mid-sentence. "Let him think what he wants about me." In a swift motion Zach stuffs my father's money in the front pocket of his jeans and my heart thunders, knowing this is his way of telling my father to fuck off. "He is The Judge, after all."

The Judge narrows his eyes and raises a pointed finger at Zach, ready to fire threats like he always does when he's challenged. I grip my man's side preparing for my father's wrath.

I hear my mother gasp and my mouth hangs open just before her body goes limp and she collapses to the floor. She was never good with conflict, passing out at anything the slightest bit stressful.

"Honey?" My father lands on his knees next to my mother's side holding her head up while my brother uses his medical training to assess her.

Zach and I stand in my family's foyer wrapped together in a show of solidarity. No matter what they say, I'm going to be with him. Like he said earlier, it's him and I against the world. If my parents don't want to support that, I might have to make one of the most difficult choices I've ever had to face and cut them out of my life.

Chapter Two

Zach

The third time her cell phone rings, Aubrey shuts is off and tosses it in her purse. She closes her eyes and leans her head back against the headrest. Her long auburn hair falls over her shoulders in full waves while her mouth pulls into a slight frown. Getting in the car with me and leaving her family behind wouldn't have been easy for her. I can't imagine telling some of the most important people in my life to fuck off because they don't approve of the person I'm in love with, but I'm glad she did. It's got to be the hardest thing in the world for her. I swallow hard as I think about how it's possible she might hate me for the little stunt I pulled.

I reach over and thread my fingers through her delicate ones while I readjust my hand on the wheel. "It's gonna be alright, babe. Give them time to adjust."

She bites her bottom lip to try and keep it from quivering. "How can you say that after how they treated you? I hate them."

I bring her knuckles to my mouth and kiss them gently. "No you don't. You're angry right now. I'm used to people treating me like that. Before I became 'Riff' days like today were what my life was like. People, especially ones with money, would watch me like a hawk, thinking in their head I was a thief and a low life."

"Didn't you hate that? Being treated like a criminal?"

I glance over at her beautiful questioning face. "It wasn't exactly a fucking picnic, but I get that some people don't understand rock culture and tattoos are just another outlet for us to express creativity."

She looks down at her lap. "I'm sorry."

I reach over and tap her chin up. "What are you sorry for, Kitten?"

Aubrey sighs. "For everything. For the shitty life you led, for the way people treated you and above all how *my* family treated you. I expected so much more from them. I thought they would at least have enough faith in me to trust *my* judgment and see you are a great person—someone I love."

I pull into the first decent hotel I see and park the Fusion. I pivot in the seat and turn her face in my hands and force her to look at me. "No one has ever stood up for me like that before—chosen me over basically their entire world. It means a lot that you did that, but I also want you to know even if they treat me like shit, I always want you to have a relationship with your family."

"Zach, I won't have anything to do with them if they don't accept you."

I stare into her green eyes. "They don't have to accept me, Aubrey. All that matters to me is that *you* do. You know my darkest secrets, and all the fucked up details that make me who I am, and you haven't run for the hills screaming. I'll do anything for you. *Anything*. I want you to be happy and I don't want you to fight with your parents over me. I don't want you to resent me one day."

A tear leaks from her right eye. "I would never resent you. Ever."

I brush away the fallen tears from her face with my thumbs and lean in to press my lips against hers. "I love you, Kitten. I'll always treat you right."

After I pay for a room at the front desk, we take the elevator up to the fifth floor and roll our luggage down the hall to our room. I swipe the room card and open the door, ushering my girl inside. It's a typical king-sized bedroom, with neutral walls and white bedding.

Aubrey flops down on the bed and kicks off her shoes. Her bare legs dangle off the side, and the green dress she's wearing rides up her thighs as she stretches her arms above her head. She's fucking beautiful and perfect. There's nothing about this girl that doesn't turn me on. Instantly, the need to hold her in my arms overwhelms me and I can't help but give in to it.

I remove the hat I'm wearing and toss it to the empty chair in the room before I crawl into bed next to her. On my side facing her, I prop my head up with my left hand and stare down at her. I trace the bare skin on her left shoulder before slipping my fingers under the spaghetti-strap holding up dress. It hooks with ease around my index finger and I slide it down, exposing the top of her left breast. A white lacey bra covers her nipple, but I pull my fingertips down the curve of her breast and feel its silky-softness. My cock jerks in my jeans from the simple contact and almost as if she knows how fucking turned on I'm getting she smiles the most perfect smile.

Aubrey opens her eyes and brings her hand up to my cheek, touching it softly, and I turn my face into it, kissing her wrist and inhaling the sweet scent of her perfume. Before her I was lost, constantly at war with myself. I didn't believe I was worthy of a love so simple and pure. It's something I still battle with, but with each passing day I grow a little more at ease with having something so great in my life. I fucking love this woman, and there's nothing I wouldn't do for her. Aubrey and my band are all that matter to me in this fucked up world.

"What are you thinking?" she whispers as she stares into my eyes.

I lean down to kiss her lips, and the necklace I'm wearing rests on her chest. "About how lucky I am to have you."

She bites her lip. "I was just thinking the same thing."

"Liar," I say and then kiss the tip of her nose.

She pulls my mouth back down to hers. "Let me prove it to you."

"You'll get no arguments from me, babe."

Her leg swings around and hooks on my hip as she pushes her weight against me, throwing me back against the bed. Long strands of hair frame her face as she straddles me and shoves my shirt up in order to rake her nails down my abs.

I suck in a quick breath from the amazing feeling of pleasure and pain it creates. "Fuck."

I sit up, wrapping my arms around her before crushing my lips to hers and plunging my tongue in her mouth. A soft moan vibrates out of her mouth and I feel the sound it makes as I deepen the kiss. My hand runs up her back and then threads into her thick hair. My dick strains against my jeans, begging for entrance into my most favorite place on the planet—buried deep in her pussy.

She tosses her head back and I drag my lips down her neck to her collar bone. "God, Zach. I want you."

It's all the invitation I need to take her. I yank her dress and an audible tearing sound fills the air as I rip the top down exposing her breast. Kitten doesn't seem to notice because she's too busy pulling my shirt over my head. I love how fucking excited she gets when I touch her.

She circles her hips, rubbing her panty covered pussy against the fabric of my jeans. The pressure of her body against mine makes my cock throb and I can't take it any longer.

I shove her dress up over her hips, rip her panties off her body, and then run my fingertip over her swollen clit.

"I actually liked those." I don't have to look at her face because I can tell from her sultry tone that she's pouting.

"I'll buy you fifty fucking new ones. They were in my way and had to go," I say against her skin and she giggles.

Feather-light kisses caress my shoulder as I kneed her tits. Her taut nipples rub against my chest as I grab her face and kiss her hungrily. The only word that float through my sex-hazed brain is *mine*. How this woman will always be *mine*.

My index finger slips inside her. "Damn, Kitten. You're always so ready for me."

"It's because I always want you," she breathes into my ear.

I slip my hand away from her body and flip her onto her back. "That's good to know because I always fucking want you, too." I grab her hand and guide it to my stiff cock. "You do this to me. Just the thought of sliding into you causes this. I love being inside you."

She bites her lip as she sits up and makes quick work of freeing my dick from my jeans and boxer-briefs. Her wet tongue darts out from behind her teeth and she licks my shaft from root to tip on both sides while she stares up at me, watching my reaction.

Her lips wrap around me and she swirls her tongue around the head before taking even more into her mouth. The warmth of her mouth causes a tingle to erupt all over my body and I shudder from the pure delight.

I sweep her hair to the side and hold it back as I watch her work. The sight alone nearly makes me come in her mouth. "Damn, baby. You're so fucking good at that."

I suck a quick breath in through my teeth when she looks up at me and says, "I need you inside me."

As much as I want to make that happen for her, I shake my head. "I believe in fair play."

Before she can say another word I grab her hips, yank her ass to the edge of the bed and kneel down. I spread her thighs open and then use my fingers to open her folds to expose her swollen clit. I circle my tongue around it and taste the sweet juices of her arousal. I fuck her with two fingers while using the trick of drawing a figure-of-eight with my tongue to work her into a frenzy. She grabs handfuls of the comforter at her sides as she cries out and screams my name. Her pussy clenches my greedily around my fingers as she rides the wave of her orgasm.

Her body goes limp as I stand and guide my cock into her. "Mmmm. I'll never get tired of fucking you."

I shove into her down to the base and then pull back out, loving how wet she is. I wrap one of her legs around my waist and props the other up on my chest as she leans up on he elbows. "Oh, Zach. That's it. Right there."

I love it when she lets me know I'm pleasing her. Mutual gratification is always the goal when I'm making love to her.

My fingers dig into her hips as I pump faster while she stares up at me with hooded eyes and her mouth hanging open. Our eyes stay locked as warmth spreads over my body. I try to fight it off and think about something else, but it's fucking impossible with her looking up at me like that—all sexed-up and panting.

I feel myself slipping into sweet oblivion, and I know I can't hold back much longer. Aubrey's brow furrows and her mouth pulls into an 'O', and I nearly loose my mind as I know she's about to find bliss with me with time. "That's it, baby. Come for me." She closes her eyes and cries out my name. "Shit," I growl.

A whimper escapes her as she lets go at the exact time I do. Heat pulses through me as I fill her full. I love coming inside her. I never knew the difference wearing a condom made until I experienced raw sex with Aubrey that first night. Now, I'm fucking addicted to it, just like I am this amazing woman beneath me.

It takes a second for the nerves in my body to stop twitching and for me to regain my composure. Aubrey grins up at me while biting the tip of her manicured fingernail. She's fucking adorable.

I bend down and kiss her lips. "I fucking love you, do you know that?"

She laughs. "I have a pretty good idea."

I move my hips and slide my still semi-erect cock in and out of her. "This should give you a great fucking idea. I'm already gearing up for round two."

Her lips crush mine. "You really are a machine."

"Damn straight, babe. I'm ready to make you scream all night long."

She shakes her head and grabs my shoulders pulling me down and then rolling onto of me. "It's my turn to take control."

With that I lay back and enjoy the show while my woman fucks me like there's no tomorrow.

"Shit!" Aubrey exclaims as she turns her phone on. "Ten missed calls from my mother and three from Gabe."

"Maybe you should call them back. They're worried about you," I suggest.

She shakes her head. "They should be worried about me ever speaking to them again after the way they treated you."

I can't argue with her much there. The Judge have might as well punched me square in the balls and placed a restraining order on me to stay away from his daughter with the way he acted towards me. When he slapped that money in my hand, it took everything in me not to shove it down his throat and tell him I wipe my ass with more. I was pretty proud that I was able to keep my temper in check and merely shove it in my pocket once he found out I was with Aubrey, and not some fucking servant.

Gabe seems pretty cool though. "Why don't you at least call your brother and tell him the tattooed deviant didn't steal you away and murder you. That should ease your mother's mind and keep her from passing out again."

Kitten sits next to me on the bed and frowns. "I don't know what's come over them. They've never been such…"

"Assholes?"

She answers with a sad smile. "Yes, assholes. I'm sure it was a lot for them to take in. They're not used to me being with someone who looks like you."

I nod thoughtfully and my mind drifts back to the reason we came here in the first place. "You mean they'd much rather see you with that douchebag, Isaac?"

She rolls her pretty green eyes. "Someone *exactly* like him."

"You know, Kitten, meeting them really makes me understand why you were standoffish in the beginning and only wanted a fast fuck from me."

"It does?" I hear the question in her voice.

"Of course it does, but it also shows me how much you care about me—about what you're willing to risk to be with me." I push a lock of hair behind her ear. "I love you, babe."

"I love you, too."

She turns the phone over in her hand and I can see how hard fighting with her family is for her. My heart squeezes at the thought of her pain, and I'll do anything to bring a smile back to that pretty face.

I nudge her arm. "Call them."

She shakes her head again.

"At least call Gabe."

Aubrey sighs and turns the phone over to stare at the screen. "I guess it won't hurt to call him."

I give her another little nudge. "Go on."

Her fingers fly over the keys and then she places the phone up to her ear, waiting for a familiar voice on the line. "Hey…I know, but…really?" She turns toward me with wide eyes. "Maybe…No…No promises, Gabe. If they act like that again, I'm done…All right. I'll talk to you soon."

Anxious to know about the other side of that conversation, I try and coax some information out of her. "Sooo…what's going on?"

"They want us to come back over for dinner. Gabe says they want to apologize and start over now that the shock of the situation has worn off."

I tilt my head to the side. "You know, I was thinking about something."

"What's that?"

It's a hard subject to broach, but it's something I need to know. "Why would you so blatantly defy them to be with someone like me?"

Aubrey stretches her hand up and glides her fingers from my cheek to my earlobe. "Being with someone like you was never in the plan, but I can't help that I find your bad-boy ways so damn appealing. I know that wanting to make a life with you is seriously against the rules, which is why I only wanted to keep our relationship to one night. But you grew on me and I couldn't drag you out of my heart no matter how hard I tried. The more I'm with you, the more I want you. I love you, Zach. For some crazy, messed up reason you're my soul-mate. The man I'm supposed to be with forever." She looks away from me. "I really can't explain it without sounding like a total girl. It's like fate brought you and I together."

I lean down and brush my lips against her shoulder. "I feel the exact same way."

She gazes into my eyes and blinks a couple times. "You do?"

"Of course I do. Now, get some clothes on and let's go give your family the do-over they want. I promise not to hold your father's dickhead actions against him."

She nods. "I wouldn't blame you if you did."

"He's your pops, babe. I'll suck it up and try to reel in the asshole gene that I love to display just as long as he doesn't fucking push me."

Kitten's lips pull into a lop-sided smile. "Thank you."

Thirty minutes later, Kitten and I are parked in the same exact spot in the driveway. For some strange reason, I feel the nerves getting to me. Even being on stage in front of thousands of people doesn't make my hands feel clammy like this.

What the fuck is wrong with me? It's just her dad. I've told executives and big shots who call themselves in charge of the band off before, which could've flushed the bands career down the toilet, and never felt like this.

I risk a glance at Aubrey and she's chewing on her lip. "Hey." I touch her hand. "It's going to be a lot better this time."

She sighs. "I hope so." Her eyes flit up to the house and then back to me. "Ready?"

"As I'll ever be." I hop out of the car, not giving her any more time to dwell on the what-if's.

She opens her door before I have a chance to make it over to her and steps out of the car. A timid smile crosses her lips before she grabs my hand in hers and tugs me towards the front door.

The second we step onto the landing the door swings open and her brother greets us with a grin. "That was quite the show. I'm really glad I came back for this."

Aubrey rolls her eyes. "You look for any excuse to get out of school. Tell me again how you're managing to make it through med school?"

"Ha. Ha. You think you're funny, don't you?"

She pinches his cheek as she passes him, and we step through the threshold. "I'm only joking. I know if you didn't take that year off to go back-packing through Europe with me you'd be done by now. It put us both behind in school, but it was totally worth it."

I furrow my brow. "You never told me you did that."

Gabe pats me on the shoulder. "How long have you two been together?"

I pause as I think about that question. Our relationship has been so crazy up to this point I can't honestly give him an answer. "I'm not sure."

He chuckles and shakes his head. "Sounds like there's a lot you two don't know about each other. Come on, everyone's sitting down."

He's right. I'm sure there's tons of shit we don't about each other yet, but that doesn't change the way I feel about her. She's amazing, and that's enough for me. The rest will come with time. I'm sure of it.

Chapter Three

Aubrey

My father stands the moment Zach and I enter the room. "Hi, honey. Thank you for coming back over."

Before I have a chance to answer, Mom swoops in out of nowhere and wraps me in a hug. "Dear, thank you for coming back. I'm sorry for that little scene earlier. You're very important to your father and I, and we don't want to drive you away by not accepting your…lifestyle. Forgive us?"

"Mom, it's not a lifestyle. I'm not becoming a deviant. Sometimes first impressions are incorrect." I step back and cling to Zach's side. "Mom, Judge, I would like you to officially meet my boyfriend, Zachery Oliver."

The Judge's lips pull into a tight line as he extends his hand out to Zach. "Sorry about before, son. I'm Charles Jenson and this here is Connie." He tilts his head in Mom's direction.

"It's good to meet you both," Zach answers and I smile, silently thanking him for being so gracious.

"Come on, now. Everyone have a seat and let's eat," Mom says.

Once we're all seated at the expansive table in my parents elegant dinning room, Anna serves salads and fills the glasses on the table with water. Zach removes his hat, revealing his crazy hair and both of my parents' eyebrows instantly shoot up. I can tell it's killing them not being able to say something about the hair, but they know they're treading on thin ice here, so they hold it in.

The Judge sits at the head of the table, unfolds his dinner napkin and clears his throat. "So tell me, Zach. What do you do for a living?"

"Daddy..." I warn, wanting him to know not to cross the line.

"Calm down now, sugar. It's a respectable question any father would ask a man his daughter brings home. I just want to get to know the boy is all."

Zach pats my leg under the table and I instantly relax a bit. "It's a perfectly legit question, Mr. Jenson."

My father interrupts him. "Son, feel free to call me Judge. Most people round these parts do."

I grip Zach's hand and give it a squeeze so he knows no matter what he tells him or what they say, I'm with him.

"Well, Judge, I'm actually a musician. I play—"

"I knew it!" Gabe nearly shouts. "That's where I've seen you before. You're the guitarist for Black Falcon! Hot Damn!"

"Gabriel!" Mom scolds my brother. "We don't use that type of language at the table."

"I'm sorry, Mom, but this is Riff from Black Falcon—one of the biggest bands in the country." Gabe stares at Zach dreamily with his mouth still agape. "I bet you pull women left and right. What are *you* doing with my sister?"

My mother studies Zach with curious eyes, awaiting an answer and no doubt mentally calling my boyfriend a manwhore while she waits. "How nice, you're a celebrity. It sounds as though congratulations on your success are in order."

Zach presses his water glass to his lips and takes a sip. "Thank you, Mrs. Jenson. My band has been really lucky to catch the breaks we have to get us to the level we're on."

My father swallows down his salad and then directs his attention towards Zach. "Is it safe to assume there's quite a bit of traveling involved with being a professional musician?"

Needing to take some of the pressure of the firing squad off Zach I interject. "There is, but luckily he has enough pull to get me backstage whenever I want."

"What's it like back there? I bet the women are insane," Gabe says.

"Pull yourself together, Gabriel, and act like you have some sense. You're acting as though you were raised by wolves. The type of women that hang around those events aren't for you." Mom's doing her best to keep her cool, but I can see the thought of her son indulging himself in a horde of groupies is going to cause her to lose it.

Gabe wipes some salad dressing from his mouth. "Your daughter was one of those women. They can't all be bad."

I choke on my water and my eyes grow wide. "Hey!"

"Actually, I met your sister during a business meeting when she worked at Center Stage Marketing. She was working on a project with us, along with Lanie Vance." I smile up at Zach, thanking him for saving me a little bit of face with my family.

"You're in the band that the boy Lanie married is in?" Mom's finally starting to make the connections of how I ended up with a rock star.

"Yes, ma'am. The very same."

"I couldn't help noticing you said when she worked, as in past tense. Something you want to tell us, Aubrey?" I glance over at my father and tension instantly overtakes every muscle in my body.

Explaining to my family how I threw everything away in order to be with Zach is not going to go over well. They take careers pretty seriously, especially my father.

I stare into my father's gray eyes. "That's actually what I came home to talk to you about. There was a complication with my job, and well, I got fired. I need your legal advice on getting my job back."

"Fired? When?" My father asks.

"Last week, right around the time of Lanie's wedding."

Mom's mouth pulls into a tight line. "Aubrey Jenson, why didn't you tell us about this right away?"

I shrug. "Because I was embarrassed and didn't know how to. The reason I was fired has nothing to do with my work performance, but rather whom I'm dating, and well, I didn't want to exactly tell you about all this over the phone."

My father narrows his eyes at Zach. "How did dating this boy cause you to lose your job?"

Zach's hand squeezes mine and I swallow hard as the thought about revealing my truth. "I...uh...I was sort of dating my boss."

"Aubrey!" I can hear the gasp in my mother's voice.

My father leans back in his chair and begins poking around at his salad—no doubt pondering how to approach the subject. "Honey, I do believe you have legal grounds upon which to seek reinstatement, or in the very least, a case for wrongful dismissal."

I sit up a little straighter in my seat and smile. "Really? That's great. Do you think if you called them—"

He holds his hand up, effectively cutting me off mid-sentence. "As much as I would like to help you, I can't get involved."

My eyebrows pull in. "Why not?"

"Because I'm your father and I'm a judge now. It wouldn't be in the best interest of the case for me to represent you since the nature of the case is...complicated."

My shoulders slump. "Oh."

"But," he continues, "There is a new attorney that I know that would be great at assisting you. He's hungry to take on cases like this. I'll give him a call right after dinner."

I finally dig in to my salad, feeling at ease that my father seems somewhat understanding. "So is the guy someone from your old firm?"

My father chews his food and nods thoughtfully. "He is, and you actually know him."

My mind flits back to the few times I'd met his colleagues. All of them are qualified to help me figure this thing out, but none of them are new. I have faith Dad wouldn't steer me in the wrong direction. "Which one is it? Larry or Steve?"

"Brady Larson."

The smile instantly drops off my face and my eyes grow wide. Is he kidding me? He's recommending my high school boyfriend?

"What, darlin'? You look like a deer caught in the headlights."

I glance over at Zach. His head tilts towards me as he studies my face and panic hits me. I don't want to have secrets between him and I, so I might as well get everything out on the table. "Brady is my old boyfriend from high school."

A light of recognition sparkles in Zach's eyes. "It's okay, Kitten. I don't see anything wrong with him taking your case."

"Y—you don't?" I stumble over my words, completely shocked that he's taking all this so calmly. "You're okay with that?"

He takes my hand and kisses my fingertips right in front of my family. "Me and you against the world, right? I don't have anything to worry about, do I?"

I shake my head as I stare into his eyes. The transition he's undergone since the first time I met him is amazing. The womanizer who handed out golden tickets to groupies to avoid any type of real relationship is a world away from the man sitting beside me now, but we're still working on trusting one another. I want to reassure him he has nothing to worry about. "Of course not."

The Judge clears his throat. "Now, then, since that's settled, let's talk about what else you've been up to."

We finish the evening chatting about different aspects of our lives, and Zach even manages to make my mother smile every now and again with his witty charm. My father doesn't fool me, though. I know he's watching my man for the slightest crack of weakness to exploit. He didn't get to be where he is today without going to any length needed to get his way, and in this case I know he despises the fact that I'm dating a man like Zach. It was obvious the moment he mentioned Brady taking my case. But no matter if he does, I'm not leaving Zach. That much I'm sure of.

"So, Zach, do most of your friends call you Zach or Riff?" Gabe asks as he works on the apple pie Anna set in front of him moments ago.

Zach's eyes slide to me and he smiles. "Aubrey is the only person who really calls me by my given name. Everyone else is happy to call me Riff."

I bite my bottom lip and think about that first night together when he insisted I not call him Riff. I should've known I was special to him at that point, but with a reputation like his, it was easy to believe I meant nothing to him. Boy, how wrong was I?

"Is it cool I call you Riff then? I think the name is pretty bad-ass."

Zach smiles. "Sure."

"Sweet. Promise me you'll come to the club with me sometime. Having you as a wing man will increase my pull with the ladies." Gabe glances down at his watch. "Speaking of which, I got to go."

I snicker. "Ah, yes, the crushing appointments."

Gabe stands and then slides in his chair. "You're one to talk about crushing."

My mouth gapes open, and my brother winks at me before scooting out the door to meet up with some little, snobby socialite-type.

A scraping noise drags my attention to my father as he pushes back from the table and throws his cloth napkin on the table. "I'm going to go give Brady a call and set something up for you."

I nod and smile. "Thank you."

Dad stops as he walks around the table and places his hand on my shoulder. "You're my baby girl, darling. I'll do anything to protect you."

The smile on his face seems genuine and while I know my father loves me and wants the best for me, I'm not sure we exactly agree on what that is.

Mom blots the corners of her mouth with her napkin. "Aubrey, honey, since you're here I wondered if you'd accompany me to find a new dress for Larry and Dee Hanigan's anniversary party at the club this weekend. Maybe we can pick one up for you as well. They'd love to see you."

"I'm really not sure how long I'll be in town," I answer, trying to get out of what I know will be a boring party for my parents' friends. "We should really be getting back to the hotel."

"It's only six, surely you don't have to rush off so soon?" There's almost a pout in her voice.

"Mom...Zach's here and it would be impolite to leave him alone."

Before I can further express all the reasons I can't go, Zach speaks up, "It's fine, Aubrey. I can hang out here for a couple of hours while you spend time with your mother. I have my laptop out in the car. I'll grab it and handle some band stuff while you're gone."

I study his face to see if he really means it or not. Maybe he wants a little break from me for a while or something. "If you really want me to go, I'll go."

He slides his hand up my thigh, and the urge to jump his bones comes to mind. "It's fine. We have all night to hang out."

I don't miss the hint in his subtle words and it makes my pulse race to an embarrassing level, knowing I have eyes directed on me from across the table. "If you're sure it's okay."

I silently pray that he changes his mind and decides to take me back to the hotel. I drag my nails over the back of his hand and his eyes hood a little.

He blinks slowly and sighs. "I'll be fine. I'm not going anywhere."

"Good then, it's all set. I'll go grab my purse and we'll head out." Mom's delighted voice snaps me out of the dazed stupor Zach and his sexiness put me in.

The moment we're alone in the dining room Zach grabs my face and crushes his lips against mine. "Don't be gone long."

I trace his bottom lip with my tongue. "Now, I'm definitely tempted to tell her I'm not going."

His face lights up with a crooked grin as he sucks on his lip ring. "As much as I would love that, you can't. She'd be disappointed now."

"What about you?" I can hear the whine in my voice.

"I'll be fine. It'll be good to check in with the guys and see what's going on. Besides, I've neglected my fan page lately. I really should get on that."

"Don't go and text random women who message you." I'm kidding...well mostly, anyway.

Zach laughs and kisses me softly. "You're the only fan I want dirty messages from now."

My face heats up as I recall how our relationship began with a string of texts promising hot sex. "Good to know."

After a couple more kisses, I grab a post-it note and pen from the kitchen to write the Wi-Fi information down for him, and promise not to be gone more than a couple hours. He just grins and encourages me to spend time with my mother, reminding me how sometimes life is too short so I should spend all the time I can with her.

My heart sinks a little knowing what he's been through with his sister and his mother. I need to suck it up, take his advice, and make the best out of buying a stuffy dress.

Chapter Four

Zach

Seven hundred and thirty-seven messages? Holy fuck. That's what I get for not keeping up with this fan site. This is going to take me a month to sort through. I lean back on the brown leather sofa and close my eyes, completely overwhelmed with the amount of work to do. I'm tempted to say fuck it and take a nap instead, but I know that's not fair to the fans. This is their outlet for their passion about my work. How can I ignore that?

I take a deep breath, grab a snack pack of Oreos from my bag and then get to work. It's a painstakingly long process, but to see their giddy responses when they realize I've replied personally make it all worth it. Before Aubrey, this was the place I came to feel love. My fans poured it out to me unconditionally and I soaked it up. That's actually why I started bagging so many groupies. There's nothing like being someone's everything.

"You got a minute, son?" I glance up from the computer screen to find the Judge leaning against the doorframe into this impressive den. "There's something I would like to discuss with you."

I glance down at the clock on my computer. Damn. I've been answering messages for an hour and a half and didn't even realize it. Aubrey should be back soon, but I wonder why her father wants to talk to me without her present.

Fuck. This can't be a good sign.

I swallow hard. "Sure."

I stand and follow Judge down a short hall into an office. There's a very classic look in here, with chocolate walls, cherry bookcases and a matching desk. There's even a bottle of Scotch, accompanied by four glasses, sitting on a side table.

The Judge's eyes follow my line of sight. "You want a drink?"

This is probably some sort of test on his part. If I accept the drink, he'll automatically think I'm a partying alcoholic, but if I refuse, he'll think I'm lying.

"Sure," I answer, but don't plan on drinking the entire thing.

He walks over and removes the glass cork from the Scotch, pouring two glasses half-full. After handing me a glass, he walks around his desk and sits in the high-back chair. His eyes study me intently as we sit in silence, staring at one another.

Judge sits the glass on his desk and leans forward in his chair. "I'm not a man to beat around the bush about things, Zach. I'm very direct, and I don't keep what I want secret. If more people were like me, the world would be a better place. We would all know where we stand with one another."

This sounds like the intro to a speech about him not liking me very much. Instead of starting an argument with the father of the woman I love, I simply nod my head like I'm in total agreement. I could be wrong about him, after all. I barely know the man. "I like directness."

"Good, because I'm about to lay it all out for you."

Oh fuck.

"Why are you dating my daughter?"

That's an easy answer. "Because I love her." There's no waiver whatsoever in my voice as I speak my truth.

He stares at me a long moment before he continues. "I can see that you believe that, but I know your type—the here today and gone tomorrow guys. I have to be honest with you, Zach. I don't want that for my little girl. She's too good for that. She deserves a man that's stable and isn't going anywhere."

I flinch, but understand his reservations. My past isn't a favorable one. "I can assure you when it comes to your daughter, sir, I'm not going anywhere."

He sighs. "I was afraid you'd be stubborn about this. You leave me no choice."

He slides a print out of some sort towards me. "What's this?"

"Your sealed record."

My eyes grow wide as they scan the record of my historical brushes with the law. "How did you get this?"

He frowns. "I'm a judge, son. I can get access to anything."

"But, why do you have it? Aubrey already knows about all this. You telling her won't stop her from being with me."

He nods in agreement. "That's true, but the press would have a field day with something like this, wouldn't they? It'd be a shame if this was leaked somehow."

I shoot up from my seat, sloshing my drink around before I slam the glass down on his desk. "Are you threatening me?"

His eyes grow wide for a second and I can tell for a split second I've rattled his tough exterior. "Calm down. This could be a threat, but I would prefer to think of it more as a bargaining tool."

"What do you mean—a bargaining tool? What do you possibly stand to gain by smearing me across the press?"

"My daughter."

I shake my head. "She wouldn't leave me over that."

"No, probably not. My daughter is fiercely loyal—gets that from me, so she'll stick by your side. That's why you're going to leave her."

"No! There's no way in hell I'm going to leave her. She'll understand."

"She may, but I took the liberty of pulling the other band members' histories as well. Trip Douglas appears to have some dirty secrets too. I don't think Trip would appreciate his secrets being shared with the media, or being made public. If you don't walk away from Aubrey, then you're going to force my hand. I'll tear your band apart."

My pulse races under my skin, causing my hands to shake. Was I really such a bastard this man would ruin the lives of other people to keep me away from his daughter? Can't he see I'm a changed man? I fucking worship the ground Aubrey walks on. I'd never hurt her. Why would he try to stop a love so pure?

"Why? Why would you do this? I told you I love her. Isn't that enough?"

"No. It's not. I want her with a man who I know will always take care of her. I'm not getting any younger, and I don't want to leave this earth with the fate of my daughter in the hands of some young punk who'll ruin her life at some point."

"I won't do that. I have more than enough money to give her an even better lifestyle than this place if she wants it!"

"For now you do. What happens in ten years from now when your band breaks up and the money stops? What then? You going to drag her down with you?"

His words feel like a fucking smack to the face. He's right. I have no other skills. None. Music is everything to me. I'll never stop doing it, even if I don't make another penny for it. It's in my blood. I can't give it up.

The other thing that kills me is the fact that he's right. While Black Falcon is on top of the fucking world right now, I know that won't last forever. There's always another fame-hungry band ready to out-rock you and steal your fans. God knows we've taken enough breaks and cancelled enough shows to leave half our fans pissed off. What happens when I can no longer give Aubrey the life she deserves?

"I'm going to take your silence as confirmation that it's sinking in? You and I both know she's not the girl for you. She needs to be with someone like Brady—a guy with his head on straight, and a solid future. You shouldn't be selfish and stop that from happening for her."

I pull my eyes up from the floor and stare at him. I have no doubt he'd smear both me and Trip to the press if given a chance. While we know about each other's pasts and have moved on, it doesn't mean the rest of the world will.

I sink my head into my hands. As much as I love Aubrey, I don't want to be the one to hurt her someday. I don't want her to resent me. She deserves the best life she can possibly have—the nice house, a husband home every night, kids.

God. Kids.

The last part stings the most. I've never let the fact that I can't have kids bother me before, but knowing I can never give her something like that fucking kills me.

The thought of Aubrey pregnant, with a soft glow, smiling as she carries my baby inside her taunts me like a nightmare—one that, no matter how much money I have, will never be fixed.

I sigh, knowing that deep-down I'm still a fucked-up loser who doesn't deserve my red-headed goddess. "What do you want me to do?"

"I want you out of her life. For good."

"I can't just leave her here. She'd expect an explanation, and I don't want her to know what an evil dick you are. It would ruin her whole perception of you."

He laughs bitterly. "Very well. Finish out the weekend here, and on Monday I want you on the first plane out of Texas and forget she doesn't exist."

My lips pull into a tight line. "I might be on a plane, but you'll *never* make me forget her."

I don't give him a chance to say anything else before I storm out of the room, grab my computer and head for the car. I can't stay here one more second and listen to him tell me that he's ripping the one thing I care about in this world away from me.

I toss my shit on the passenger seat and crank the car alive, nearly squealing the tires as I back pull out onto the street.

I rub my forehead vigorously as I come to a red light. "FUCK!"

My entire body shakes as it hits me that once again I've lost everything that's important to me. The light turns green just as my eyes burn and tears stream down my face.

Anger wells inside me, and I pound the steering wheel with my hands. "Fuck. Fuck. Fuck. Fuck. FUCK!" I scream at the top of my lungs.

How is this happening? This isn't what's supposed to happen. It's me and Aubrey against the world. I should go back and tell him to go ahead and tell the fucking world I killed my family. It wouldn't matter if he did. I'm nothing without her anyway.

I slam on my breaks ready to turn around and the car behind me blares its horn, pulling me back to reality. I can't go back. That would make me a selfish prick, just like the Judge says. I'd destroy Trip, probably royally fuck the band, and never allow Aubrey the chance to have a baby.

I take a deep breath and mash the gas. I can't be here anymore. If I can't have her, I can't see her. I won't be able to play it off that everything is fine. She'll know. She'll see how fucked up I am.

I park the Fusion in the hotel lot and head to my room. I let myself in and stare at the rumpled sheets on the bed, picturing her naked body laying there, begging me to take her. My chest constricts and suddenly I find it hard to breathe. I crawl into bed and bunch the sheets up in my arms, burying my nose in the soft cotton as I inhale her scent.

"I'll always fucking love you," I whisper, doing my best to picture Aubrey in my arms.

The next thing I know someone's pounding on the door. I shake my head and stare down at the sheets and pray the last few hours of my life was a fucking nightmare. I drag myself out of bed and yank the door open.

Aubrey's face twists the moment she sees me. "Really, Zach? You couldn't wait on me?"

I sigh and close the door behind her. I'm a fucking idiot to think I wouldn't have to see her again. All her shit's here. "I'm sorry alright. I was tried and you were taking forever."

"I was only gone two and a half hours. I thought you were okay with waiting. If you didn't want me to go, all you had to do was say so." She crosses her arms over her chest and waits for me to apologize.

More than anything I want to. I want to tell her I'm sorry for thinking I could have her—that I'm worthy of her. But as I stare into her eyes, all I feel is shame for the hurt I know I'm going to cause her soon.

She frowns and closes the distance between us so she can touch my face. "What's wrong?"

I glance over at the bed and lick the corner of my mouth, fighting the sting in my eyes. I can't let her see me break. "Nothing. Just tired."

"Did something happen while I was gone?" There's a slight inflection in her voice. "The Judge trying to scare you off? Because if he is, don't let him. No matter what it is—I won't care. I love you."

I open my mouth to tell her exactly what her father is trying to pull, but quickly close it. I don't want to be the reason she never speaks to her family. God knows I wish I still had a family to be close to.

I close my eyes and lean my forehead against hers. Can I really give this up?

"Zach, you're scaring me. Please tell me what's wrong."

Shit, this isn't going well. I need a distraction. If I keep on thinking about this I'm going to drive myself insane.

Without warning I wrap my arms around her and pull her into my chest and kiss her like it's the last time I'll ever get to taste these lips. Her eyebrows rise for a second, but she quickly relaxes into me and grabs my neck. I hate keeping shit from her. I want to be honest, but I can't. I have to keep this shit to myself and figure out how in the hell I can make all this go away and still keep her. I'm not ready to let this go, not by a long shot.

Chapter Five

Aubrey

This kiss feels different. It's almost desperate, like he's clinging to me for some reason. I wish he would tell me what's wrong. If I had to guess I would say my father has gotten to him—pushed his buttons in some way and that scares me. We've struggled so much to get to this good place, and I don't need someone interfering and putting crazy ideas in his head.

Zach's nose skims my cheek before he nips on my earlobe. "I need to be inside you. I need to feel you."

The dress I'm wearing falls to the floor before I have time to ask him any more questions. All I feel is his warm mouth on my neck, licking and teasing the sensitive skin below my ear. If he wants a distraction, I'll give him the best damn one he's ever had.

My hands slip under the hem of his shirt and I push it up, ready to feel his skin against me. He grabs the back of shirt and drags it over his head in the sexy way that men do. The defined muscles in his chest clench under my touch. His sister's name, Hailey, etched into the flesh above his heart makes my heart squeeze thinking about what he's been through in his life. I lean in and kiss the tattoo before going down further and swirling my tongue around his taut nipple. I take my time grazing my teeth against it, teasing him before dropping to my knees.

After I make quick work of getting his jeans down around his hips, I tease the tip of his length with my mouth before going straight for the kill. My gag reflex kicks in when his head touches the back of my throat.

Zach tangles his fingers in my hair. "Jesus, fucking, Christ. You keep that up and I'll come down that pretty throat of yours."

Knowing I make him feel so good pushes me to keep this up. I pick up the rhythm and I cup his balls. He emits a low growl and I know he won't be able to hold back much long if I don't stop.

I stare up at his hooded eyes. "I want you to fuck me now."

The tip of his tongue flicks across his bottom lip. "Bend your sexy ass over the bed." A thrill shoots through me as I comply with his demand. Zach unhooks my bra, slides it over my shoulders and it falls in front of me on the bed. The distinct rustling behind me of Zach throwing his jeans and underwear to the floor causes me to start to turn around. "Don't move. Your ass looks delicious like that."

Before I can argue any further, Zach drops to his knees behind me and sinks his teeth into my panty-covered ass. I cry out from the wicked combination of pleasure and pain. This is what makes sex with him amazing—he's always doing shit I don't expect.

One hand grips my thigh while the other presses against my soaked panties and my entire body shakes. "Always begging for it, aren't ya?"

"Only from you," I manage to say with a straggled voice.

A quick slap on my ass makes me jump. I wasn't quite ready for it, and it startles me a bit, but at the same time I want more. "Mmmm."

He chuckles darkly. "My little naughty girl." He raises and leans himself over my back, pressing his rock-hard cock against my ass, so he can whisper in my ear. "You want me inside that pussy?"

I suck in a quick breath as he slides my panties aside and runs his finger down my wet folds. "Yesssss."

"Then tell me, Kitten. Does this pussy belong to me?" Of course. What would even make him question that at this stage of our relationship? "Tell me, baby. Tell me this is *my* fucking pussy. I want to hear you say it. I want to know you're mine. All mine. That this will always be mine."

I try to process what exactly he wants from me and why he suddenly needs to stake his claim on me. This extreme possessiveness is new. Before I have a chance to answer his finger slips inside me. "Oh, God."

"You want more of that?" he whispers roughly. "Say it and I'll fuck the hell out of that sweet little pussy for you."

Every inch of me quivers with need for him. I'll say anything he wants as long as he takes me now. "It's yours. It's always been yours."

"Damn straight," he growls and rips my panties completely off. "Don't forget it, either. No matter where I am or what happens between us, your body belongs to me."

He spreads my legs further apart and smacks my wet folds with his fingers—not hard enough to hurt, but hard enough to make me moan like I'm in heat. I'm pretty sure if we have any neighbors they know I'm about to get my brains fucked out.

All of his fingertips rub in a circular motion around my clit, but never touches it directly, robbing me of the pleasure I need. I arch my back, trying to push him into touching my sweet spot, and I'm met with another little slap. "Always so greedy. I want to take you to the edge and keep you there in sweet agony. The moment I do finally allow you to come, I want you to remember it's only me who makes you feel this good."

I growl a little in frustration, loving yet hating this game as his cock slides against my pussy. I close my eyes and bite my lip when the tip of him hits my clit. It's a deliciously slow pace. A small bead of sweat forms on my upper lip. The salty taste falls to my tongue when I lick my dry lips. All this panting is revving me up even more.

If he keeps this up I might be forced to throw him down on this bed and take matters into my own hands.

"I feel how much you want this. Your need is covering my cock. You're so ready for me, aren't you?" His hot breath covers my cheek and I shiver. "I'm dying to be inside you. Balls deep in you, babe, is my favorite fucking place on earth. It's just as hard for me to hold back."

"Please, Zach," I plead. I'm so fucking turned on by him I can't see straight. Typically we get right to it—we're both very much instant gratification people.

His mouth covers my shoulder as he continues to tease me. "Please what, baby?"

"Please fuck me," I answer honestly.

He moves to the other shoulder, tasting my skin along the way. "Please fuck what?"

I throw my head back and shudder when his tip touches my swollen clit. This is still about making sure I remember I'm his. He still wants to hear me say every part of me belongs to him. "Please fuck your pussy."

He growls and lightly bites my shoulder, sliding his cock into me. "That's what I fucking want to hear."

I cry out, screaming his name followed by a yes, as he finally starts giving me what I so desperately need. "You feel so good."

"That's because we're meant to be. This body was made for me." His thrusts pick up speed.

My sex clenches around him greedily, trying to hold him deep inside. I can't take much more. "Zach, I—"

"I know what you need, baby. We're going to do this together. Hang on." He grips my hips tighter and begins to pound into me. "Fuck."

Zach grabs my hair and then twists, wrapping it around his wrist. My head pulls back just as he reaches between my legs and flicks my clit. "Oh, God. Zach." The words no sooner leave my lips as every inch of me fills with warmth. A euphoric orgasm washes over me, at the same time Zach growls my name as he finds his own release.

He lays his chest against my back. "I fucking love you. I'm not going anywhere," he mumbles with his lips pressed to my skin.

I turn towards him and touch his face, completely confused on why he feels like there's a problem between us. "Who said anything about either of us going anywhere?"

His green eyes meet mine and he shakes his head. "No one. Forget I even said that. It was the post-sex haze talking. You make me lose my mind."

I smile at him because I know exactly what he means.

The ringtone on my cell phone pulls me out of a deep sleep. I roll over and look at the clock on the bedside table. Who the hell is calling me at seven thirty in the morning?

I grab my phone to check out the screen. I sigh and swipe the answer button. This could be important. "Hello, Judge."

"Good morning, honey. Sorry to call you so early, but this just couldn't wait. I spoke with Brady this morning and he's willing to take on your case." My father's voice is just too damn chipper for this early in the morning.

"That's great. When can we go see him?" I sit up in bed and rub my eyes.

"We? Wouldn't you rather handle this matter alone?"

I furrow my brow. What a ridiculous thing to say. Zach came with me down here. Of course I want to involve him. "No. Zach and I have no secrets."

The Judge clears his throat. "Well you see, darlin', I told Brady that you'd be meeting him for lunch. He said he'd make reservations for the two of you at that little French place the two of you used to go to when you dated. Wouldn't be fair to him to bring along another man to that place, would it?"

"Daddy," I scold him. "Brady would be my attorney, handling a legal matter for me. This wouldn't be a date. Where would he even get the idea that it might be?"

He's quiet for a few moments. "I might've encouraged the idea a little, but that was only to get him to take your case."

Unbelievable! I shake my head and stare up at the ceiling. "He would've taken the case anyway and you know it."

"You're right. I just figured maybe you could use a little…space, is all."

He just doesn't get it. I know Zach isn't the kind of man he'd choose for me, but he needs to know I'm serious about him—that we're solid. "Where I go, Zach goes. I don't need any space."

He sighs. "Maybe you don't, but I've got to say the boy seemed like he wanted a little space from you yesterday when we chatted."

My heart squeezes in my chest as I stare down at my beautiful boyfriend sleeping beside me. He wanted space? "He said that?"

"Not directly, no. He didn't have to. A man like that doesn't settle down long. They're wild and the call to roam and stray always tugs at them. Maybe it's best to create some space between you the two of you now to avoid the heartache later. I just don't want to see you hurt anymore. Your momma can't take it—tears her up every time you call crying."

I rub my forehead. What the hell is going on? Is that why Zach didn't wait on me yesterday? Does he seriously want me to give him a break? Have I been too blind to see any signs that my man's unhappy?

Maybe I shouldn't force him to go see Brady with me. Maybe Daddy's right.

"What time does he want to meet?" I ask.

"He'll be at the hotel to pick you up around eleven thirty."

I nod and readjust my back against the pillow. "I'll be ready."

"Good girl. He'll have some great advice for you. Brady's smart and I trust him like he's my own son. He'll point you in the right direction. I have no doubt." I roll my eyes, catching the subtleties of how much my father likes my old boyfriend.

"Okay, thanks. I'll call you later and let you know how it goes," I say just before we say our goodbyes and make plans to meet for dinner later that evening.

I stay in bed running through what my father said. Now that I've had time to process everything, I think my father's full of shit. There's no way Zach's tired of me already. He wouldn't have come here with me. He's too straightforward for that.

Zach stirs next to me and rolls over to towards me. He opens one eye and peeks up at me. "You're awake already?"

I study his handsome face and nod. "I've been up for over an hour now."

He wraps his arm around my waist and closes his eye. "What for? Can't sleep? I get that way in some hotel beds too, but this one is pretty comfortable."

I shake my head. "Been up thinking."

"'Bout what?" He snuggles into my side.

"About you leaving me." His body goes rigid next to me.

"What makes you think that would happen? Didn't I make that pretty clear last night that you're mine?" His tone sounds a little annoyed.

Things still don't make sense. Something else is missing. Something both Zach and my father are keeping from me. "You did, but my father's under the impression that you might not be sticking around. Care to tell me what went on between the two of you while I was gone?"

He lets out a heavy breath against his pillow. "Nothing went on, babe. Your father just doesn't like me very much."

I rest my hands on the arm that's around my waist. "So the impression I just got from my father that you're ready to leave me to run off and fuck a slew of groupies. Is that the truth or just his wishful thinking talking?"

"Babe, I'm too selfish a man to leave you, even if it's the right thing to do. I'm fucking addicted to you and there's nothing anybody can do that would make me give this up. I've decided."

I slide back down under the covers and snuggle into my man's arms. Instantly, I feel silly for even considering the idea that he's unhappy. We're obviously still solid. Guess I'm going to have to have a chat with the Judge about trying to interfere with that.

Chapter Six

Zach

I've decided Aubrey Jenson is my fucking kryptonite. The smart thing would be to take The Judge's warning seriously and leave the girl the fuck alone, but I can't do that. Last night only reminded me how much I fucking love this woman. She's mine and no one is taking her away from me. I don't give a fuck what the cost is to keep her. Trip's just going to have to deal if his shit blows up—just like I will.

I lay on the bed and watch Aubrey pull a brush through her thick, red hair as she gets ready to go and meet with Brady. I want to hate the guy since I know he's the first man to ever have tasted of her sweetness, but I can't—not if he's going to help her get back the job she wants so desperately.

I am curious about him though. "So what's this dude that we're meeting like?"

Aubrey stares into the mirror. "He's a nice guy. Cocky, but generally a nice guy."

A nice, cocky guy? That's the equivalent of the high school quarterback type with a lot of money—a douchebag in my book. I'll probably want to kick his ass in the first five minutes.

I clear my throat. "If he was so nice, why'd you break up?"

She sighs as she opens her lip gloss. "He's older than me. I was still in high school when he was in his junior year of college. There was just too much of an age difference to stay together back then. We were at different points in our lives."

I raise my eyebrows. If this fucker had better things to do than to keep a beautiful woman like Aubrey on the back burner back then, I don't want him trying to take care of her now. I'm worried he's not worthy to be the one to get her what she wants. This woman is my world and I'll do anything to make sure she's happy. "Maybe we should reconsider hiring him."

She glances over at me with a smirk, expecting I have a smart-ass remark to follow that. She knows me so well. "Why's that?"

I shove myself off the bed and move into the bathroom to stand behind her. I grip her slender upper arms with my hands. "Because the asshole must be crazy if he let you go." I lean in and kiss her cheek. "How smart can he really be?"

Kitten smiles. "Smart enough to know he was never going to be man enough for me."

I smirk. "That's right. You have a thing for the bad boys."

She turns in my arms and places her hand over my heart. "Only bad boys with hearts made of gold."

There it is again—her believing the best of me. I wish I could believe her—that deep down I'm a noble man, but only hours ago I was willing to walk out on her for my own selfish reasons. Granted, I'm still not happy about The Judge dragging Trip into this fucking mess, but I figure the only reason he did that was because he knew I would tell him I didn't give a fuck if the world knew about my history. I don't give a shit what people think of me. I only care about her. Aubrey is my world now, and damn it, I'm keeping her—no matter what.

Aubrey taps my forehead with her index finger. "Whatever you've got going on in that crazy brain of yours, don't doubt you're a good man."

I sigh and stare into her green eyes before I cup her face in my hands. "What did I ever do to deserve you?"

She drums her fingers against my chest. "You gave me this."

I press my lips to hers and get lost in how much she means to me. Like always, I'm turned on by her slightest touch. "I'd like to give you a whole lot more if we had the time. It's a good thing our ride will be here any minute, or otherwise you'd already be naked and beneath me begging for me to be inside you."

Her breath comes out in ragged spurts and I know she wants it, just as much as I want to give it to her.

Almost as if on cue her ringtone goes off, filling the silence in the bathroom.

She leans her forehead against mine. "That's probably him now."

My hands fall to her waist. "Are sure you don't want to reconsider staying here with me? Like I told you before, you don't have to work. I'll take care of you."

She shakes her head as she picks up her phone and swipes the answer button. "Hello?"

I sigh and kiss her neck, trying my best to distract her.

"Hi, Brady. I know. It has been forever...we're ready...oh, I'm sorry, my father probably forgot to tell you. My boyfriend's here with me...okay, we'll be down in five minutes." She ends her calls and pushes me back a little. "Do you know how hard it is to have a conversation when you're licking me like that?"

I grin. "Probably about as hard as it is for me to keep myself from throwing you down on that bed and not letting you out of this room."

She rolls her eyes. "You're impossible. He's downstairs waiting for us."

I push her auburn hair over her shoulder. "Well, let's go if we have to. The sooner we leave, the sooner we can get back."

I wiggle my eyebrows at her and she laughs. God, I'd do anything to hear her laugh like that all the time.

We make our way outside the hotel's front door to find a white Audi R8. I study the car's smooth flowing body-work and let out a low whistle. "This is a nice car."

"It's really pretty," Aubrey says.

"Pretty? This thing is a V10, babe. There's nothing *pretty* about this thing, it's a bad-ass beast. Calling it pretty insults it," I say.

She shrugs. "It's just a car."

I'm pretty sure my ears are bleeding. I can't believe she called this fine piece of workmanship *just* a car. Being a man into speed, I know my cars. Most men would give their left nut for this. "Kitten, this is a dream car. I'm sure some spoiled shit-stain owns it and babies the fuck out of it. What a waste."

Before I have a chance to say anything else, the passenger door pops open and a man gets out.

"Brady!" Aubrey's voice holds a little too much excitement for my liking. "Wow! Look at you."

The man smiles at her and removes the dark sunglasses from his face, before shoving his brown hair away from his forehead. His eyes lock on my girlfriend and his gaze travels down the length of her body, lasting a little too long on her tits. My fingers curl into tight fists at my side. "Aubrey? Oh, my God. Aren't you a sight for sore eyes? You've grown up well."

This is going to be even worse than I thought. This is a well-off, pretty-boy douchebag—just the kind of man The Judge wants his daughter to be with.

Kitten rushes around me to greet Brady the moment he steps around the car and his feet land on the sidewalk. I know I said I wasn't going to be jealous, but damn if I don't feel a little twinge of it eating at me inside. When I see them hug, I instantly want to pull them apart, and punch him in the face.

I'm so lost in thought I don't even hear Aubrey introduce me. I'm brought back to reality when Brady extends his right hand to me. "I'm Brady. It's good to meet you, man."

Our hands clap together. "What's up? I'm Riff."

Aubrey raises her eyebrow at me, and I know it's because I introduced myself with my stage name. She and her family call me by my birth name, but I would prefer the general population stick to the other. Aubrey and her parents calling me Zach reminds me to keep things real with them.

Brady stares down at Aubrey. "You ready to go? We have a reservation in fifteen minutes."

"Sure," she says. "I'll sit in the back."

Both Brady and I stare at the sports car in front of us.

"Babe, this car doesn't have a back seat," I tell her.

She twists her berry-stained lips. "How are we all going to ride over to the restaurant? Can we follow you, Brady?"

Brady scratches his temple. "That's the other thing. I only made the reservation for two and it's lunch time, so I'm not sure if they'll be able to accommodate a third person. I wish your father would've told me you'd be bringing a guest."

Immediately I feel like I'm imposing. While I'm sure Aubrey would love for me to go with her, I'm sure she can handle this on her own. I trust her, it's this fucking pretty boy that I have an issue with. He can't keep his fucking eyes off her. I know that look of wanting to stick your cock inside a woman. I've perfected that fucking look.

I sigh and fold my arms across my chest. Brady's wide eyes trace the patterns of my ink, and I can tell it makes him a little uncomfortable. I smirk. "You two go on ahead, babe. I'm sure you can take notes and fill me in on the game plan when you get back."

Kitten places her dainty fingers on my arm. "Are you sure? I don't want to leave you out. We can always go somewhere else."

I shake my head. "I'll be fine. We're only talking an hour or so tops. I'll find something close to eat and wait over at your parents' house, okay?"

She frowns. "I feel like shit for leaving you out."

I lean in and kiss her forehead. "I trust you."

She smiles and promises not to be too long, as Brady opens the passenger door for her. The moment he shuts her inside the car and turns toward me, the smile drops off my face. Brady's eyes widen as he takes in my curled lip. He races around the car—nearly tripping off the sidewalk in the process—to get the hell away from me.

I should feel bad for scaring the guy, but I want him to know not to fuck with something that's mine.

He speeds off a little faster than I approve of, which is probably my fault. Both of my arms drop to my side as I head out to the parking lot. I know she doesn't need me for everything, but I still like to be there for her. The rental car pulls out smoothly onto the busy street and I turn into a local fast-food Drive-Thru to order some food. My cell phone buzzes as I sit in line.

"Fuck," I mutter to myself as I check the caller ID. So much for him leaving me the hell alone. I hope to God he isn't calling for more money. Two million dollars should've lasted him longer than a couple weeks.

On the third ring I take a deep breath and answer. "What?"

"Hello, I'm trying to reach Thurston Oliver's next of kin," a strange man's voice says on the other end of the line. "The contact on his phone says 'son', but doesn't give a name. I'm hoping you're the son of Mr. Oliver."

I stiffen in my seat. "Yes, I'm his son."

"For the record could you tell me your name?" This dude sounds very formal. No way he's a bookie or something.

I clear my throat to keep it from closing completely shut. "Zach Oliver."

There's some paper rustling around on the other end. "Mr. Oliver, I'm Officer McCurry. I'm sorry to be the one to tell you this, but at ten thirty-two this morning the hotel maid here at the Hard Rock found your father deceased in his hotel room. By all indication he's been dead for a few days. When was the last time you spoke to your father?"

Even though I hated the bastard, my insides crumble. The only family I have in the world is gone. Any connection I had to my past is gone…just like my family. Gone.

A silent tear leaks down my cheek and I bat it away. "It's been a few weeks since I've talked to him."

"Do you think you can come identify his body? We'll need to send him out for an autopsy to confirm the cause of death, but by the looks of his room it appears to have been an overdose," the cop informs me.

Stupid asshole. Why would Dad start messing with drugs and shit? Didn't he learn anything when he was dealing with me and my addiction back in high school?

I lean my head back against the seat. This is partly my fault for trying to pay him off. The least I could do is go out there and ID the body and bring him back to be buried beside Mom and Hailey. "I'll get a flight out as soon as I can."

"Great. Stop by the Las Vegas Police Department and ask for me when you get here."

I nod, even though I know he can't see me. "All right."

The moment the phone call ends, a horn blares behind me. I pull around and get out of line, suddenly not hungry any more. I dial Aubrey's cell but it goes to her voicemail.

Shit. I need to find her.

I find myself on her parents' street. The Judge knows where she is. I'll ask him how to get to the restaurant.

The front brakes squeal a little when I jerk the car to a stop in the driveway. I leap from the car and make it to the heavy, wooden door in record time. My fist stings as it beats against the door.

A few seconds later the housekeeper, Anna opens the door. "Mr. Oliver, is everything all right?"

It's then I notice how hard I'm breathing and it's taking everything in me not to come across as a total nut-job. "The Judge here?" Anna furrows her brow and nods. I can tell when she takes a step back she isn't sure if she should let me in. I want to reassure her I'm not here to cause any trouble so I smile at her. "Thank you."

Without even knowing why, I instantly head back to the office where The Judge threatened me last night and burst through the door.

The Judge glances up from the stack of papers on his desk and jerks his glasses off his face. "What in the hell do you think you're doing?"

"Tell me where Aubrey is," I demand without further explanation.

He pushes himself up and stares me down with his gray eyes. "I'll do no such thing. I thought we had an understanding last night, son. You're going to let her move on. Why on earth would I tell you where she is so you can barge in there like a maniac and ruin things for her? I won't allow you to scare Brady off."

"Too late for that. I already made sure that uptight fucker knows Aubrey is my girl. No way he'll have the balls to make a move on her now. So tell me where she is!" I feel my body shake as adrenaline courses through my entire body. If he's smart, he won't push me right now.

Her father studies my face. "You aren't going to be as easy to get rid of as I thought, are you?"

I shake my head. "I'm not going anywhere, so you might as well learn to deal now."

His body stiffens and he crosses his arms. "I don't have to learn to deal with anything. Now, I suggest you walk your ass out of my office before I call the police."

"Tell me—" I stop mid-sentence as he picks up the phone. The police coming here after I've made a scene won't be a good thing. It's bad enough that the press will probably catch wind of my father's overdose, so I don't need to add fuel to the fucking fire. "Fine. I'll drive around until I find her on my own."

I turn and storm out of the room just as fast as I entered. I thread my fingers around the back of my head and growl in sheer frustration. My voice echoes through the large foyer, making me sound like some kind of rabid beast. More than anything I want to punch something hard. It takes every ounce of my strength not to turn march back in there and shove my fist in The Judge's smug face.

I fling the front door open and once I'm outside, inhale deeply through my nostrils. "Fuck!"

"Yo, bro. Everything alright?" I jerk my head toward Gabe's voice. He stands in his driveway with a sponge and bucket beside what I assume to be his car.

I shake my head. "I need to find Aubrey."

He sets this bucket down. "She's not with you?"

"No. She's with Brady at some restaurant, and your father won't tell me where to find them. I have to speak with her. It's an emergency," I say.

"Do you know which restaurant it is?"

I nod. "Some place they used to go to all the time in high school."

Recognition registers on his face, and Gabe rubs his hands together, dusting them free of a few soap bubbles. "I haven't started to wash her yet. Come on. I'll show you how to get there."

Finally I have someone willing to help me. Relief washes through me. "Thank you."

Gabe nods curtly. "Let's go."

Once we're a couple miles down the road, I allow my mind to wonder about my father and what his last few moments on this earth was like—if our family was the last thought he had. A familiar pang of guilt fills me as I allow the blame of his death to fall on my shoulders as well as my mother and sister's.

I grip the steering wheel so tight my knuckles start turning white. Gabe glances over at my hands and then up to my face. "Everything okay, Riff? You seem tense. Did you and Aubrey have a fight?"

A sigh escapes me. It's so fucking hard to talk about my family. Aubrey is the only person that's got me to open up. That's why I need her right now. I need her with me. I have to hang on to the last thing I have left in this world with both hands—to hell with the Judge. If wants to destroy me, let him fucking bring it.

I finally shake my head. "No. Aubrey and I are great. There's just been a…death in the family. I need to leave right away."

"Oh, man. I'm really sorry. Were you close to the person?" Gabe questions, genuine concern in his voice.

I swallow hard and feel it's best to be honest as I can be with him. "Not really, but I'm the next of kin and I have to identify the body."

"Ouch, that's rough. Were they your uncle or something?"

I keep my eyes focused on the road in front of me and concentrate on keeping my emotions in check. "My father."

I'm glad when Gabe doesn't press me any more on the topic, and he continues directing me to the restaurant. "Pull in the valet station. It's the only way to park in this city."

I hop out and toss the valet the keys. "Leave it here and keep it running. I'm not staying."

Soft piano music and the smell of fine Italian food waft through the air, while the over-dressed wait staff scurries about with trays of food. Jesus, this is where they hung out in high school? That shit-stain Brady must have a loaded family too.

I crane my neck around the hostess podium to get a good look at the dining room. My eyes sweep the room, landing on the back of Kitten's red hair. I take a couple of steps in her direction, but the tall, slender hostess with long dark hair steps in front of me. "Can I help you, sir? Do you have a reservation?"

There's no way she's stopping me from getting to my girl. "This will only take a second. I'm not staying."

"I can't let you go in there looking like that." The woman rakes her eyes down my body with a sneer of disgust.

I glance down at the t-shirt and jeans I'm wearing and roll my eyes. "I said I'm not fucking staying, so move."

I don't stick around to argue with this chick. Nothing she says is going to stop me from walking the last ten feet before me to get to Aubrey.

"Sir…you can't. Please, sir—" I hear the woman's voice behind me fade into the distance. All that matters now is getting to my world.

Two seconds later I pause mid-step as I get close enough to see Brady's hand resting on top of Kitten's. Brady's arm stretches across the table and he's massaging the side of her hand with his thumb. My blood boils instantly. How the fuck can she do this to me? Doesn't she know she's my fucking world? How can she let that ass-wipe paw her like that?

We've been apart less than a fucking hour and she's allowing this to happen? How am I going to trust her when I'm on the road for months on end? I can't believe I was stupid enough to believe this relationship was fucking real.

I clench my fists by my side and step directly behind her. "Having a nice lunch?"

Aubrey's gaze leaves Brady's face as she whips her head in my direction. Her eyes widen, and she knows she's been caught.

Chapter Seven

Aubrey

The look in Zach's eyes scares the shit out of me. It's wild and unpredictable. A snarl pulls across his lips as he glares at my hand on the table. Instantly, things click.

I immediately shake my head. "No, no, no. It's not what you think."

His eyes cut to me. "You mean you weren't holding your fucking ex's hand in the middle of some goddamn fucking fancy restaurant."

The curse words spewing from Zach's lips cause an old lady at the table beside ours to gasp and grab her chest, while a mother with her small son on the other side covers the kid's ears. A couple of the wait staff stop mid-stride and stare in our direction.

This is about to escalate really fast. When Zach's pissed his emotions completely take over, and he goes into a physical rage. The broken furniture in my apartment can attest to that.

I stand and face my man. "Let's talk outside."

He folds his arms over his chest. "You don't want to bring your new boyfriend with you?"

I narrow my eyes. "He's not my fucking boyfriend."

Zach glares back at me and flexes his jaw. "Could've fooled me."

My nostrils flare as I suck in a deep breath. "Outside. We need to talk." I turn to Brady, who is still seated in his chair looking like a frightened squirrel. "Thank you for lunch and the advice on suing Center Stage, Brady. I would like to go ahead and start that process."

Without saying another word I storm out through the restaurant. Tension rolls down my back as I feel the heat of the judgmental stares burning into my back until I make it out the front door. The rental car is sitting out front, the motor still running. Gabe's face twists the moment he sees me. So that's how Zach knew how to find me. I always knew he was a jealous man, but I never thought in a million years he wouldn't trust me for even an hour and a half. I can't believe he's making such a big fucking deal about this. Brady was only showing me a little support as I poured my heart out to him, explaining that both of my parents hate my boyfriend and believe he's no good for me.

I yank open the door and slide into the back seat, still fuming that Zach felt the need to act like a dick and embarrass me like that.

"What's up, sis? You look pissed," Gabe says turning around in his seat. "You okay?"

I roll my eyes. "I don't get what his problem is. He stormed in there like a lunatic, and practically announced to the entire restaurant that I'm cheating on him with Brady. I don't know where the hell he gets off."

It feels good to vent to my brother. I need a neutral party in the situation.

Gabe's face pulls into a lopsided frown. "The guy's having a pretty hard time. His—"

Before Gabe is able to finish his sentence, Zach swings open the driver's door and flops into the car. Daggers shoot from my eyes into the back of Zach's head as he pulls onto the street and heads north to my parents' place.

The entire ride is silent and I don't like it. I want to scream and cuss at Zach for the way he just treated me back there, but having Gabe in the car with us stops me. I don't need to drag my brother into the middle of my fights.

Over and over in my head I play out the scene of how our fight is going to go down. The moment he opens his mouth to yell at me for something I didn't even do, I'm going off on his ass. He isn't going to treat me like that.

We pull into my parents' driveway and Gabe immediately gets out of the car and heads into the house. I stay in the back, ready for him to start—hopefully with an apology.

Zach sighs and rubs his hand over his face. "Get out."

I flinch. "What did you just say to me?"

He turns to face me with hard eyes. "I said…GET. OUT."

A gasp leaves my mouth and my bottom lip trembles. "Zach…"

He closes his eyes. "Aubrey, get the fuck out. I'm done with you. It was a mistake to think a relationship with you could ever work."

A sob escapes me. "How can you say that to me?"

His eyes meet mine. "Because you're just like the rest of the sluts I've ever been with. Always looking to trade up when you can."

"It's not what you think, please." I hear the desperate plea in my own voice as I beg him to not do this. "Please don't ruin us."

"Do not make me physically throw you out of this car. I don't want you." I search his face for a sign, for anything to tell me this isn't really him talking, but there's nothing. The stone cold look in his eyes makes him appear dead inside.

I swallow hard as I open the door. My eyes automatically go to the ground when I step out and shut it behind me. I can't believe this—over, just like that. He didn't even care what I had to say. It was like he was a man possessed.

The tires on the Fusion squeal when they make contact with the asphalt and he drives out of my life. My entire body shakes and my knees buckle, causing me to fall into a puddle on the driveway.

Tears fall without warning as all the built-up emotion bursts out of me. My chest squeezes and I gasp for breathe. I can't breathe. I'm suffocating. I gasp for air but no relief comes. I'm dying, I know it.

Hands shake my shoulders and a paper bag is shoved against my mouth. "Breathe, Aubrey. You need to calm down."

Gabe's commanding tone takes me by surprise and I automatically obey him. I hold the bag around my lips and breathe into it. After a few seconds the pressure in my lungs eases up.

Gabe smiles down at me. "That's a good. You're going to be all right. Now, tell me what the fuck just happened."

I shake my head and pull the bag away. "You're going to make a great doctor."

He pats my head. "Nice try, little sister. Flattery won't get you out of telling me."

I shrug. "Zach came into the restaurant at the worst possible moment. I was telling Brady all about the hard time The Judge has been giving Zach, and how Mom tried her damndest to talk me out of dating him when we went dress shopping."

"Go on," he insists.

"Brady sort of reached over and put his hand on top of mine and Zach saw it, flipped the fuck out in the restaurant and made a scene. I was mortified. Then we get here and he won't talk to me tells me to get out of the car and he's done with me." Another sobs comes. "And now we're over."

Gabe sits beside me on the ground and wraps me in a hug. "He didn't mean it, I know he didn't. It's just the grief talking."

I sniff and pull back to gaze up at his face. "Grief? He told you about his mom and sister?"

Gabe's brow furrows. "No. He just found out his father died."

My eyes widen "What?"

"That's why we were coming to find you. He needs to leave tonight to go identify the body."

I swallow hard and things instantly start falling into place. I knew those horribly evil things he was saying couldn't possibly be from the real him. That's the kind of fucked up shit Riff would say, not my Zach.

He needs me. He came to find me in his biggest time of need and the first thing he saw was another man touching me. The thoughts in his brain can't be rational right now.

I shove myself up off the concrete and dust my hands off. "Where are Dad's car keys?"

Gabe stands beside me, concern etched into his face. "Do you think it's wise to go chasing him down in your current state?"

"If I don't go after him now, I might lose him forever. I love him and he needs me." The thought of never seeing his beautiful face again scares the shit out of me.

My brother smiles. "You better go get him then. Dad's keys are in the drawer in the kitchen."

I grab my brother's face and kiss his cheek before I sprint into the house. Most siblings fight like crazy, and while I'm not saying we don't have our fair share of fights too, we get along like best friends who like to pick on one another. I'm grateful for that.

My parents look up from their lunch when I rush into the large black and white kitchen. I yank open the cabinet drawer that's closest to the garage without saying a word to them. It's partly their fault that this is all happening, so I don't exactly feel the need to ask their permission before I grab the keys to my father's Cadillac CTS-V. Both of my parents watch me as I allow the door to swing shut and I stalk towards the garage.

"Aubrey, honey, you mind telling us where you're heading off to in such a panic?" the Judge asks from behind me, effectively stopping me in my tracks.

My lips pull into a tight line as I pivot on my heel. "If you must know I'm going to see Zach."

My father puckers his lips. It's the signature move he makes before he hammers out something that he believes to be factual truth. "I don't think that's wise. The boy's no good for you, honey. I know you might not be able to see it now because you think so much with your heart and emotions, but someday, when you're older, you'll thank me for helping get rid of him."

"You helped get rid of him? What the hell does that mean?" My words rush out, almost like a snarl.

"Language, Aubrey Jenson!" Mother scolds with a frown on her face.

Unbelievable! "Fuck my language, Mother. Some help you two are. You're ruining my life, don't you get that? If I lose Zach, my world is over."

"I'm your father. It's my job to protect you and look out for your future," Dad says as he wrinkles his brow.

They still don't get it. I better make this clear for them. "Zach is my future. You two either accept that or you won't have to worry about seeing me again because I'm never letting him go."

This time when I head for the door I don't stop, no matter how loud they yell and order me to come back.

I hop into my Dad's most prized possession and tear out of the garage the moment the doors open. Heading for the hotel, my brain replays everything that just went down in my parents' kitchen. I know they're pissed at me, but they're going to have to get over it. I love Zach, and nothing is going to change that.

My thoughts drift to Zach and I pray that he'll hear me out. I want him to see my side of the situation and understand that I did nothing to betray his trust—that he's my everything.

I shake my head and sigh as I approach a traffic light. In need of a distraction, I reach down and flip on the radio and begin searching the stations for something decent to listen to. Two clicks away from my favorite station a horn blares, and my eyes snap back to the road in front of me. It's not until it's too late that I realize the light was red, but I barreled on through anyway.

Something hits the car hard on my side and my head jerks right and then left before everything goes black.

Chapter Eight

Zach

I fling the last of my dirty clothes in the suitcase and zip it up. It's strange to know that in a couple hours I'll be leaving here without the girl I love and will never see her again. How stupid was I to believe what we had was real? I'll never shake the image of another man touching her out of my head. I always knew I didn't deserve happiness.

I scrub my hands over my face just as someone pounds on my hotel door. The only person that knows I'm here is Aubrey, but after the way I left her she'll never come here. She probably hates me. The things I said were cruel and I wish I could take them back.

The entire situation in the restaurant got out of hand. When I saw Brady's hand on hers, I flipped the fuck out. Images of rushing Brady and tackling him to the ground played over and over in my mind. It took everything in me not to do it. Poor bastard would've been leveled if he'd gotten me full force.

It probably wasn't what I thought, but knowing that Aubrey's father hated my guts coupled with the fact he was trying to take the only two things I still had left in this world—the band and Aubrey—flipped a switch inside me. Seeing Aubrey with Brady in that moment made me believe The Judge was right—she's better off with someone else, and I still belong to Black Falcon.

The person on the other side knocks again and calls my name this time. "Riff? You in there?"

What the hell is Gabe doing here? On the way to the door I glance down at Aubrey's suitcase and decide to take it with me. It's better to just hand it over and avoid any little talk he wants to have about me hurting his sister. There's no need for him to start a fight with me, defending her honor. I already know I'm a bastard.

I yank open the door and thrust the luggage out to him. "This is everything."

Gabe pushes it back towards me with both hands. "I didn't come here for here for that."

I raise my pierced eyebrow. "I hope it's not to talk, because Aubrey and I are done. There's nothing else to discuss."

Gabe shakes his head and licks the corner of his mouth like he's trying to figure out what he can say without starting a war with me. "If you're really this much of a dick, maybe I shouldn't tell you what I came here to say."

I brace my hand against the door jam. "You probably shouldn't. I like you, and I don't want this getting out of hand."

He scratches the back of his head. "If I wasn't so sure my sister fucking loves you, I'd be tempted to lay your ass out, but she does. I came here because I figured you can't be a total fucking tool since she nearly died coming to try and keep you in her life."

My chest tightens and suddenly it's nearly impossible to breathe. "What did you say?"

Gabe nods. "She's been in an accident. When I told her about your father, she picked herself up off the ground and took our dad's car to come comfort you. She ran a red light and a truck side-swiped her."

My throat closes up and I attempt to swallow to force some air into my lungs. I bend at the waist and brace my hands on my thighs and stare up at Gabe who watches me with wide eyes. My entire body shakes. "Is she alright?"

Gabe frowns and his eyebrows soften. "She's in the hospital."

I shoot straight up and grab Gabe's shoulders. "Where is she? Take me to her!"

He smiles sadly. "It's good to know you still love her, because she's going to need you."

"What do you mean?"

"Aubrey hasn't woken up since they brought her into the hospital."

I fall to my knees, the hotel door hitting my side. My girl—my Kitten—is hurt and it's all my fucking fault. I close my eyes and the tears burn trails down my cheeks. If something happens to her, I swear to God I'll never forgive myself.

I need to be with her. I need to be the one taking care of her. "Take me to her."

Gabe grips my shoulder. "Come on. I'll drive."

We grab all the luggage from the hotel room, including the guitar that I never travel without, and head down to Gabe's car. Once inside and on the road to the hospital, I catch myself fidgeting. My right leg bounces and I chew the skin on my right thumb. "Are they running tests?"

He bites his bottom lip as he makes a left hand turn. "They were doing a CAT Scan of her brain when I left."

I sigh, hating being at the mercy of a bunch of doctors to make her better. "Do they have any clue why she won't wake up?"

"No." He grips the steering wheel a little tighter. "But a lot of times when people are unconscious for that long, it's never a good sign."

There are no words to even describe the amount of pain that floods every inch of my body. This can't be real. This can't be happening.

I take a deep breath and all the times I've spent with Aubrey flash through my mind. Her beautiful smile comes into focus— how it lights me up inside in a way I thought could never be again. Every day I thank God that Aubrey came with Lanie that night to the show for Center Stage. The moment I laid eyes on her everything changed forever. She completely rocked my world and pulled me out of the haze that was my life.

Thinking of my Kitten's friend, Lanie it makes me wonder if she knows. "Did you call Lanie?"

Gabe shakes his head and I instantly fish my cell from my pocket. After a couple seconds, Noel's number rings on the other end. "Hey, brother. Enjoying your time off?"

It's good to hear Noel's familiar voice. I open my mouth, but it's hard to tell them about Kitten. If I don't say it out loud, maybe it won't be real.

"Riff? Man, you there?" Noel questions.

"Yeah…I'm here." I hear the shake in my own voice. "It's Aubrey."

"Something wrong? You sound off."

I pinch the bridge of my nose and close my eyes. "She was in a car crash."

"Fuck. Is she okay?" Concern is thick in his voice.

"She's, um, oh God." Tears erupt again. "She's in the hospital. Her brother is driving me to her now. Jesus, Noel, she hasn't woken up. If something happens to her…" I can't even finish the sentence before I sob hysterically.

"Riff, put her brother on the phone. I need to find out where she is. Lane and I are coming to you," Noel orders, and I hand over the phone to Gabe.

I drop my head into my hands and allow all the emotion I've been fighting to pour out of me. I can't go through this again. I can't loose another fucking person I love.

After Gabe gives Noel the information on where we're at, he hands me back my phone and then pats me on the back. "You have to stay strong for her, man. Just let her know you're there for her, and try anything you can think of to try and bring her around. Maybe if she hears your voice…"

I can hear the crack in Gabe's voice, before he swallows hard. I know this is hurting him, too.

We make it upstairs to the hospital room in record time. Gabe marches on through, but I pause in the doorway and take a deep breath, trying to get my shit together. I need to stay strong for her.

The soft beep of the medical equipment echoes through the room. My eyes land on Aubrey's beautiful face. A few scratches and cuts cover her face and arms. I lick my lips over and over to fight back the tears as my eyes take in the needles poking into her skin, feeding fluids into her tiny body.

I stand there frozen, unsure of what to do with myself. I want to take her place so fucking bad it hurts. She doesn't deserve this. I shouldn't have left her. I shouldn't have said the mean and hurtful things I did. Those can't be the last words that ever pass between us. They just can't be.

A hand on my shoulder startles me. I'm so transfixed on Aubrey I don't notice anyone else in the room. "Zach, honey, she needs you. Go to her. Tell her you're here."

I stare down at Mrs. Jenson as her words sink in. "What do I say?" I whisper, and I hate myself even more for not being strong enough to know exactly what to do in this situation.

"Tell her things from your heart. We need to pull her back from wherever she is and let her know there's a good reason she needs to come back to us. We've all told her how much we love her." Aubrey's mom motions over to The Judge who sits in a chair in the corner, looking pale—a shadow of the man who I fought with hours before. "But I believe it's you, Zach. You're what she needs."

Expressing myself has never been easy, and I always fuck up exactly what I want to say. Everything depends on this moment. I want her to wake up, and I want her to know how much she means to me. "Hey, Gabe. Can you bring my guitar up? I want to try something."

He gives me a curt nod. "No problem."

When Gabe rushes out of the room, I take a few steps and fall to my knees next to my Aubrey's bed. I scoop her limp hand into mine and pull it to my lips. A few tears fall and I bury my face into the bed. I don't know how long I stay like that, but before I know it, Gabe is back with my guitar.

"I'll just set it here for you," he says to me before turning to his parents. "Mom, Dad, I think we should give them a few minutes."

The Judge first shows some resistance, but takes a long look at my face and nods, allowing Connie to push him out of the room behind Gabe.

Aubrey and I are alone.

I swallow hard as I push a strand of hair back from her face. "Baby, I need you. Please wake up."

I hold my breath as I wait for her to open her eyes and smile at me just like she always does when she first wakes up, but nothing happens. I squeeze her hand harder and begin to pray, "God, please bring her back to me. I know I don't deserve her, but *she* deserves to be here. I can't go through this again. Please..." The desperation in my voice is unmistakable, but my prayer goes unanswered.

Going for another tactic I reach for my guitar, just as a short, dark-haired nurse enters the room followed by a tall, wiry doctor wearing glasses. The nurse gazes around the room as the doctor goes to work instantly examining Aubrey. She looks at me and asks, "Did her family leave?"

I nod. "They'll be back any second."

The doctor sighs as he pushes around on Aubrey's stomach and there's no reaction from her whatsoever. "I really need to speak to them about Aubrey. Can you call them and ask them to come back?"

Gabe answers on the first ring and informs me they're just down the hall in the waiting area. I explain to him that the doctor

Is in the room and wants to speak with the family and he tells me they'll be right down.

"They'll be here any second," I tell the doctor.

"Good." His brown eyes flick up to mine under his gray, bushy eyebrows. "Are you family?"

I clear my throat and debate on saying I'm family too so I can hear whatever news they have to give, but decide to be honest. "I…um…I'm her boyfriend."

He frowns and glances at the nurse before turning his attention back to me. "Then you'll want to stick around for this."

That surprises me. Usually non-family are the first to get the boot.

Mrs. Jenson walks in clinging to the Judge's arm, while Gabe trails in behind them. They all look as drained as I feel. Heavy lines mar both of Aubrey's parents' faces, making them seem much older than they had merely a day ago.

"Is there any news, Dr. Bartley?" Aubrey's mother asks with a hopeful tone.

The doctor leans back against the footboard of the bed, and folds his arms across his chest while he faces all of us. The nurse continues to work on the computer as he starts speaking, "There is news. It appears Aubrey has a slight brain bleed."

Her parents both gasp next to me and her mother clutches her chest. "How bad is it?"

"It's very small—only about five millimeters in size. The brain should be able to reabsorb that with little to no damage."

"So why hasn't she woken up?" I ask.

His gaze fixes on me. "We don't know. We hope her this coma is just temporary, and that body her body is going to taking time to heal and will kick-start itself soon. All of her vitals are stable and there are no other concerns, but I have to ask—did you know she's pregnant?"

My mouth drops open and tingle bursts open in my chest. "Did you just say *pregnant*?"

The doctor's lips pull into a tight line. "She's not very far from what I can tell—about three weeks if all the ultrasounds are correct."

I shake my head as my entire body goes numb. "That can't be. I'm sterile."

The doctor grabs a chair, motioning for me to have a seat. "Why do you think you're sterile?"

I rub the back of my neck. "I was in an accident when I was sixteen, and that's what the doctors told me and my mom."

He pats my knee. "We aren't always right, you know. Congratulations, son. Looks like you're going to be a father."

Could he be right? It's not like I'd ever tested the sterility thing with anyone else other than Aubrey. She's the only girl I've ever had any unprotected sex with, and I know once we became exclusive she stopped her birth control because I'd told there was no point in using it with me. Is it possible? We're they wrong before?

"I'm going to be a dad?" I ask timidly.

He smiles. "Yes."

It's the first time in my life I've ever felt so close to ever having something that was truly mine. I glance over to Aubrey lying in the bed, unmoving, and stare at her stomach. My kid is in there. We're going to be a family. It's crazy to know find out the same day I lost my father, I'm going to become one.

Panic instantly sets in. What if I'm not good enough to be a father? What if I fuck this up? I rest my elbows on my thighs and press my folded hands against my forehead. What if they don't make it? I begin to cry as the knowledge that I might not get a chance if Aubrey doesn't wake up.

I bat a tear away and turn my gaze to the doctor. "What can I do to make her pull out of the coma? I'll do anything. Anything."

He smiles. "Try anything you can think of. Talking to her about memories and things that mean the most to her might help bring her around."

"I'll do anything for her," I say.

"I trust that you will." He glances up at her parents. "We'll continue to run a few more tests. They'll start later on this evening if there's no improvement. Any other questions?"

They all shake their heads and the doctor excuses himself from the room.

The Judge turns to me and I instantly bolt up from the seat, ready to kick his ass if he wants to try and fight with me over this. Aubrey doesn't need to hear that.

He takes quick steps over towards me and I throw my hands up, ready to fight, but instead of attacking me like I thought he wraps his arms around my shoulders. The powerful Judge squeezes me tight as he begins to weep. "You do whatever you have to and bring her back. I know you love her just as much as she loves you. I see it. If anyone can bring her out of this, it's you. I'm sorry I gave you such a hard time before. I wanted her to be with someone who loves her."

"I do love her—with all my soul," I answer.

He pulls back. "I know you do. I understand that now." The Judge claps my shoulder and smiles at me sadly before heading for the door. "Come on, Connie. Let's give the man some time alone with our girl."

Mrs. Jenson kisses my cheek and then pats it with her fingers, before following her husband and Gabe out of the room.

I lick my lips and bend down to open the case before pulling my guitar out. I drag a chair next to her bedside and stare at her. She reminds me of a princess caught up in a sleeping spell, waiting on a kiss of true love to awaken her. Hopefully, I'm that man for Aubrey.

I strum the guitar and a song that spoke to me a lot when I was going through some major issues comes to mind. It's not until I play the first lick on the strings that I realize how fitting it is for how I feel about Aubrey.

I slow the rhythm down a bit and say, "*The Cure* helped me make it through the death of my mom and sister, but *Lovesong* takes a whole different meaning when I think about you."

My fingers slide down the neck of the guitar as I sing about how when I'm with her she makes me feel whole again. She's filled a hole in me that I didn't know was possible to fix, and made me understand that I'm worth loving. That I mean something and my life isn't just one huge fucking mistake.

I continue to sing as I think about her and our unborn child growing in her belly, and how much I need them both—more than I ever needed anything. "I will always love you."

I pick out the last few chords and set the instrument up against the wall. I stand and press my lips to hers. When she doesn't even flinch, I flop back down in the chair and lay my head on the bed. The tears start again. It's like I have no fucking control over them any more. This grief is too much to fight. The puddle on the bed grows as they keep flowing.

"Please, Kitten. I love you. Don't leave me. I can't take it," I whisper. "We're having a baby. Did you hear that? I know I might not be exactly the best father material in the world, and I'm scared out of my fucking mind that'll I screw things up, but damn it, Aubrey I want that chance. Please come back, baby," I plead with her, willing life to spark into her.

Her fingers twitch against my cheek and I jerk my head up and stare at her fingers fighting to move. I know I should call for the nurse, but I don't want to risk them coming in here and pushing her away again.

I jump up and kiss her smooth cheek. "Please, baby, come back to me." The monitor beeps pick up speed and my heart thunders. "That's it. Fight for us. Fight for our baby. Give me a chance to try and be a father—to be the man I know I can be for you."

Her entire hand jerks as soon as the words leave my mouth and I gasp—it's working. I smooth her hair back from her face. "I love you, baby—so fucking much. Don't you dare think about leaving me."

Aubrey's eyelids flutter as she struggles to wake up. "Can you hear me, Kitten? I'm right here with you. I'm not going anywhere."

The monitor's erratic pace starts slowing down as her body relaxes and she blinks slowly before she opens her eyes. Her lips part and she whispers my name, "Zach."

I grab her hand and kiss it over and over as I smile and cry at the same time. "I'm right here. I'm right here."

She nods. "It was you. I heard your voice, singing to me. It pulled me in and I had to follow it. It lead me back to you."

"I'm so sorry for how I left you. You belong with me. I'm never going to be an idiot and leave your side again. There's no getting rid of me now," I tell her. "It's you, me, and our baby forever. You're all the family I need."

She stares up at me with wide green eyes. "Our baby?"

I bite my bottom lip and hold my ring between my teeth. "You're three weeks pregnant. They found out when they were running a bunch of tests on you."

Tears leak down her cheeks. "We're going to have a baby? I thought you…"

I shake my head. "They were wrong. We're going to be a family."

As soon as the words leave my mouth, it hits me that after all these years I'm getting what I've always wanted—a family that loves me, and I love back just as much.

I wrap my arms around her and we cry together. "I love you, Kitten."

When I pull back she touches my cheek. "And I love you. Forever."

Chapter Nine

Aubrey

It's taken nearly two weeks to have Zach's father's body moved to Kentucky. It wasn't an easy choice for Zach to bury his father in the plot his family reserved next to his mother, but in the end family comes first. My man's life hasn't been an easy one. He's been through more hell than one person should ever have to withstand, but I'm glad he's finally finding true peace and becoming happier with each passing day.

The pastor says a prayer as Zach's father is lowered into the cold earth and Zach grips my hand tight. I glance over at him and watch as he struggles to hold back his emotions.

"He was a bastard," Zach says only loud enough for me to hear. "But he was still my father, the only one I ever had, and I hate that I still loved him."

I lean my head on his shoulder. "He had a lot of issues, Zach. Drugs and alcohol change people. The man you knew the last few years wasn't really your father. Don't feel guilty about loving the man you knew he really was deep down."

He turns his head and kisses the top of my head. "How did I get so lucky to have you in my life?"

I pat my stomach gently. "Us, you mean," I correct him.

Zach places his hand over mine. "It's us against the world, just like always. You're going to be a great mother."

To say I was shocked when I found out I'm pregnant would be an understatement, but it doesn't mean I love the little life growing inside me any less. I know Zach doubts his abilities involving fatherhood, but if he could see himself through my eyes he would stop all his silly doubts. He's taken such great care of me the last couple of weeks since we found out—barely allowing me to lift a finger. I grin. "And you're going to be an amazing father."

He wraps his arm around my shoulder and hugs me tightly against his side as the casket comes to a stop. The pastor motions for Zach to throw the single white rose he's holding into the open grave.

When Zach stands he pulls me up along side him and tosses in the flower. "Goodbye, Dad. I hope you find Mom and Hailey and can finally be happy again."

I sniff as his words drive home how our baby and I are really the only family he has now. That is until Noel rests his hand on Zach's opposite shoulder and Trip and Tyke stand beside him.

That's when I remember, not only does Zach have me, he has a new family in the form of Black Falcon.

"You okay, man?" Noel asks.

Zach wipes his nose on a tissue. "I'll be all right."

Noel gives Zach a sad smile and glances from Zach to me and then back. "I know you will be."

Lanie reaches around and hugs first Zach, and then me, her belly popping out a little. "Thank you for being here," I tell her.

"You're welcome, sweetie. You're two are family. I'll always be here for you. Speaking of which, make sure you're resting and drinking plenty of fluids. It's good for the baby," Lanie tells me as she pulls back.

"You'd be good to remember that, too," I remind her. "We both need be on top of our game if we're going to start this new marketing company."

"I still can't believe Diana Swagger is going to settle your lawsuit out of court. Brady must be a damn fine attorney."

I shrug. "One of the best. Besides, you know Diana. She probably didn't want a wrongful termination case to go public against her company. She doesn't like blemishes on that reputation of hers."

She nods. "Whatever the reason, I'm glad everything is working out for you. You finally have it all, girl."

There will be no argument from me on that front. She's right. I have the man of my dreams and my family seems to be coming around to accept Zach since they heard news of the baby in the hospital and *finally* figured out he's a permanent fixture in my life. Not to mention my career looks brighter. With the amount of money that Brady thinks I'll gain from the lawsuit, and the small loan I've agreed to accept from Zach, I'm looking forward to starting a small marketing firm with Lanie. Things are finally looking up for me.

We say our goodbyes to Lanie and the guys and head for the black limo that's waiting to drive us back to our vehicle. It's been a long, emotional day and I can't wait to get back to Zach's place. We are both in need of some serious rest and relaxation.

The driver opens the door as we approach and Zach helps me inside. After Zach is seated comfortably, the driver closes us in and then hops into the front of the car. Zach presses a button on the ceiling and closes the window between us and the driver.

He glances over at me. "Sorry, I wanted some alone time. I'm kind of talked out, you know."

I nod thinking back on how many extended family members showed up at the funeral. More than anything, it seemed like people came to catch a glimpse of the band than to actually mourn the loss of Zach's father. "I completely understand."

Zach turns the corner of his lips up. "That's what I love most about you. You get me—even when I don't get myself—you do. You're everything to me, do you know that?"

I take his hand in mine. "And *you* get *me*."

He stares at my face. His eyes seem like they're searching for an answer to a question that he never even asked. The ring on his bottom lip flicks in and out a couple of times as he tears his eyes away from my face and then stares down at my hand. "Fuck it. I can't wait."

I tilt my head. "Wait for what?"

His sits up straighter in the seat and untucks his button down shirt from his dress pants.

I grab his hand. "Whoa. We aren't having sex in here right after your—"

I stop mid-sentence as he grabs the hem of his t-shirt and tears a small piece of the white fabric off. I stare at him as he works on ripping it into an even smaller section and tying it into a small circle.

Afraid he's completely snapped, I ask as soft as I can, "What are you doing?"

His eyes stay trained on the fabric. "Something I should've done a long time ago." Once he's done he takes my left hand. "Aubrey, I know this isn't a real ring, but it doesn't make what it represents is any less real. You know I can buy you any ring you want—"

I gasp at his words and my heart thunders in my chest. "Zach—"

He shakes his head. "Hear me out. I know the timing of this is fucked up but the truth is, putting my father in the ground today only reminded me that we never know how much time we have in this fucked up world. And that time is precious, Aubrey. It's something no amount of money in the world can ever buy us. I want to spend every second I have left on this earth with you. I want you to marry me. Right now." His eyes stare into mine. "Let's do this. We'll drive over to the Justice of the Peace and get married. I'm committed to this family." He touches my stomach and tears roll down my cheeks. "I love you, Kitten. I want to be with you always."

I grab his face in my hands and kiss his lips, not needing to hear another word to be convinced this is the right thing to do. "Yes. I love you. Let's do this."

He slips the small cloth circle on my left, ring finger. "I'm going to spend the rest of my life showing you how much you mean to me."

I bite my lip and stare down at my hand. This homemade ring means more to me than anything he could ever have bought me because I know this comes straight from his heart. In this moment I know we are meant to be forever.

Chapter Ten

Noel Falcon

(Months later—Bonus Chapter)

I impatiently pace the lobby of the hospital, checking my watch every couple seconds. Where the hell are they? They said they would be here in twenty minutes—one more minutes than I'm going back up without them.

The minute passes and I turn towards the elevator to head back to the maternity floor, but before I get two steps away Aubrey and Riff push their way through the revolving entrance door. I let out a sigh of relief. "Thank, God."

Riff holds Aubrey's hand as she waddles through the lobby towards me. "I'm sorry, bro. We don't move very fast these days."

I take Aubrey's swollen belly. She's only a month behind Lane in due dates, so I know exactly what they're going through right now. "I get it, but Lane's about nine centimeters dilated and she's crying for Aubrey. I need to get her up there before it's too late."

Zach places his hand on my shoulder. "It's going to be fine."

I stare into the eyes of my best friend. Marrying Aubrey and both of them preparing to have a baby of their own has changed him so much. We've gotten even closer, bonding over married-life with pregnant wives together. If someone would've told me a year ago, when we were fighting all the time, that we'd be here in this exact moment, I would've called them a liar.

The elevator doors open with an audible ding. The screams of a woman in pain ring down the hall and Riff stops in his tracks. "Come on, man."

Riff shakes his head. "I think I'll find the waiting area and hang out. Keep an eye on Aubrey, would you?"

"Lane's not the one yelling like that," I say, trying to convince him to come with us.

Another loud wail comes from the open door to our right. "Just the same, I don't think it's me she wants to see."

Riff presses the elevator button and steps in as soon as the doors open.

I start after him, but Aubrey grabs my arm. "Let him go. He's freaked out because we watched a birthing video yesterday. He's afraid he'll be scared for life once he sees that with our kid."

I nod, completely understanding. "It'll be different when it's you. He'll man up. I know he will."

She laughs. "We'll see. Who would've thought bad-ass Zachery Riff Oliver gets turned into a scaredy-cat when it comes to childbirth."

I smile. "It'll be so much fun to tease him about this later."

The moment Aubrey steps into the room, Lane reaches for her and cries, "I didn't think you were going to make it."

Aubrey pushes strands of loose hair away from Lane's face. "Are you kidding me? I wouldn't miss the birth of my Godson for anything."

Lane smiles and I sigh. It's the first smile I've seen since her labor started ten hours ago. "I can't wait until my son and your daughter can play together. Have you picked out a name?"

A contraction hits Lane hard, and she closes her eyes and breathes through it. Aubrey holds her hand and counts down, watching the arc of the monitor come down. "Good job, girl. You did it."

Lane sighs and opens her eyes. "Keep talking. It distracts me. What's her name going to be?"

"We're naming her Hailey Lauren after Zach's sister and mom."

"That's so sweet."

The nurse that's been with us for the last five hours comes into the room. Her dark hair is pulled into a tight ponytail on top of her head, making her short stature seem a little taller. "How are we doing in here?"

"In a lot of pain," Lane says.

"Means you're getting close. I'm going to check you again. Hopefully you're at ten centimeters and you can start pushing. I'm going to need everyone but Dad to clear the room," the nurse orders.

Aubrey kisses Lane's forehead. "Be strong, sweetie. I'm so excited to meet him. I'll be with Zach in the waiting room." Aubrey steps to me and hugs me. "Take care of her, Dad." We laugh and I promise I will before Aubrey leaves the room.

The nurse washes her hands and slips on a pair of gloves before sitting on the edge of Lane's bed and reaching under the sheet between her legs. After a couple seconds the nurse grins. "Good news. You're ten. Let me go grab the doctor and you can have this baby."

The moment she leaves the room I drag my chair up to Lane's bedside. "I can't believe we're going to meet our son today."

She sniffs as tears roll down her face. "Me neither. I can't wait to hold James in my arms."

I wipe her tear away with my thumb. "Your dad would love that we named our son after him."

"I love that, too," she whispers.

The doctor and a team full of nurses come charging through the door, setting up equipment and putting blue gowns overtop their clothes. The doctor finally turns to us after his mask is in place and asks, "You two ready for this?"

Lane nods. "We are so ready."

I grab Lane's hand. "Let's do this."

Everything happens so fast. Stirrups pop out of the sides of the bed and the nurse that's been with us all day grabs one of Lane's feet and instructs me to do the same with the other. My eyes widen as the physician uses his fingers to massage the opening between Lane's legs as my son's head begins to crown.

Nervous energy fills every inch of me. I've never been so excited to see something so gross in my entire life.

The minutes tick by and Lane's yells out in agony as she pushes James's head completely out. "Oh, my god, Lane. You're doing it, baby. Almost there! Just a little more. I see his face. He's so beautiful."

"Okay, Lanie. One more big push to get the shoulders out, sweetheart and we'll be all done," the nurse encourages my wife. "On the count of three—push with everything you got. One, two, three…push. Push. Push. Push."

She bears down and grits her teeth. James continues to slide out, and the doctor grabs him and begins to pull at the same time. The medical staff suction his nose and mouth as both of his shoulders pass through the birth canal and a moment later our baby is completely out.

My entire body shakes as I watch them suction his mouth out completely and he begins to cry. I lean down and kiss my wife, who is just as caught up in the moment as I am.

"Congratulations! It's a boy," The doctor announces as he wraps the baby up and lays him on Lane's chest.

"Hi, James," Lane whispers. "Welcome to the world."

I lean down and kiss his little forehead. "Happy birthday, little man."

Instantly the need wish my son a happy birthday overwhelms me, so I open my mouth and begin singing the infamous birthday song.

Everyone in the room joins in and I smile as my son stares up at me with dark blue eyes, taking in the room around him. As soon as we finish singing I kiss my wife on the top of her head and thank the heavens above for the most perfect life I've been given.

Acknowledgments

I want to thank you to my dear readers for all the love for this series. It's your constant stream of support that keeps this series alive. Thank you!

Emily Snow, Kelli Maine, and Kristen Proby (aka, The Naughty Mafia) what can I say other than I flipping love you guys. You are my rocks and I love you hard.

Holly Malgieri I firmly believe we are book soul mates. Thank you for EVERYTHING! I would list it all out, but we'd be here all day and well, we both know there are too many dirty books waiting on us for that.

Jennifer Wolfel you are amazing! Thank you for the daily supporting and cracking the whip when it needs to be done.

Christine Bezdenejnih Estevez and Ellie (Ellie lovenbooks) thank you for standing by me and my books! It means the world to me. One word...VEGAS! Thanks for joining the Naughty Mafia team!

Ryn Hughes you rock my world, woman! Your edits kick ass. Thank you for all the red and I can't wait for more of it in the future.

My beautiful ladies in the Rock the Heart and Valentine's Vixen's Group, you all are the best. You guys always brighten my day.

To romance blogging community. Thank you for always supporting me and my books. I can't tell you how much every share, tweet, post and comment means to me. I read them all and every time I feel giddy. Almost to the point where I'm ready to breakout that old Sally Field speech, "You like me. You really like me," because it amazes me every time the amount of love I feel from you guys. THANK YOU for everything you do. Blogging is not an easy job and I can tell you how much I appreciate what you do for indie authors like me. You totally make our world go round.

Last, but never least the two men in my life, my husband and son. Thank you for putting up with me. I love you both more than words can express.

About the Author

New York Times and USA Today Best Selling author Michelle A. Valentine is a Central Ohio nurse turned author of erotic and New Adult romance of novels. Her love of hard-rock music, tattoos and sexy musicians inspires her sexy novels.

Find her:

Facebook:
http://www.facebook.com/pages/Michelle-A-Valentine

Twitter:
@M_A_Valentine

Blog:
http://michelleavalentine.blogspot.com/

15844113R00069

Printed in Great Britain
by Amazon